SECOND-SHOT SULLIVAN

Marshal Sullivan was a man who never shot first, but waited until the other man fired, and so far he had managed to survive. However, when Sullivan reached Estrada he found a smooth Frenchman, a fast-fingered killer gunman and a dark enchantress of a woman forming an unholy trinity against him. Determined to uphold justice, the marshal was helped by a young, loyal deputy, a golden-haired girl known as The Kansas Sunflower, and an older deputy with a liquor problem. In bringing a gang of cattle rustlers to justice, Sullivan's greatest need was to get the winning shot home.

D0638278

SECOND-SHOT SULLIVAN

SECOND-SHOT SULLIVAN

by

Jack McKenzie

Dales Large Print Books
Long Preston, North Yorkshire,
BD23 4ND, England.

British Library Cataloguing in Publication Data.

McKenzie, Jack
    Second-shot Sullivan.

    A catalogue record of this book is
    available from the British Library

    ISBN   978-1-84262-508-8 pbk

First published in Great Britain in 1993 by Robert Hale Ltd.

Published in Large Print 2007 by arrangement with
Robert Hale Limited

Dales Large Print is an imprint of Library Magna Books Ltd.

Printed and bound in Great Britain by
T.J. (International) Ltd., Cornwall, PL28 8RW

ONE

The horses pulling the stage trudged slowly up the rise and at the top prepared themselves for the easier run down the other side.

But just below the brow of the hill on the down side three riders sat facing the coach. They were pointing pistols at the driver and the shotgun guard.

A husky voice called, 'Throw down that scattergun, oldtimer. And pull them horses right up, driver. You're gunna have a little wait here. And climb down outa there, both of you.'

The driver, muttering curses but knowing there was no alternative, jammed his foot down on the brake and pulled the team to a halt.

The guard, a grizzled veteran with a sweeping moustache stained with tobacco juice, glared at the hold-up men but dropped the gun down to the ground. He and the driver followed.

The speaker urged his horse forward. He was a big hairy man, unshaven and with the face of a brute, lips thick and ugly, his eyes bloodshot and wild. The whiskey on his breath was that of cheap rotgut.

He said in a hoarse, menacing voice, 'No strong-box, I see. Well, you people in there git out. An' if you got a pocket-size pistol somewheres on you don't try usin' it. If you do, you ain't gunna make it to Estrada.'

The passengers, startled, began to climb out of the coach. One was a fat man, well dressed and with a paunch. He had the look of the banker he was. Another was a thin man with a scrawny neck dressed in a cheap suit, obviously a town man, probably a store-keeper. A third was an inky-fingered young man with the look of a bank clerk.

The other three passengers were women. They were all young but the appearance of two proclaimed them to be the saloon girls they were. Their hair was stringy and they were lean and slatternly despite their gaudy clothes and overdone make-up.

The third woman was different. She was above medium height, her hair forming a golden crest above good-looking, calm and self-possessed features. As she got out she gave the three road agents a look of complete contempt.

The big hairy man caught her glance and

sneered, 'Miss High-an'-Mighty, huh? Well, my bet is you ain't no better than these other two. You jest might be goin' to work at one of the saloons, too.'

The girl stared at him, the ice of winter in her glance. 'My profession is a little more honourable than yours. I don't rob people.'

The big man leered. 'Bet you ain't above slippin' your hand into a drunken cow-hand's pocket.'

The girl gave him another frozen look. The big man guffawed. He turned towards his two companions. One was a skinny, shifty-eyed creature with the look of a disease-ridden coyote. The other was a youth with the fresh, sun-burned face of a young farmer. He looked ill at ease.

The blonde thought quickly, his first job of this kind. That boy ought not to be riding with these two rattlesnakes. The big man called, 'Hey, Chuck, you an' the kid – git these ladies an' gentlemen to turn out their pockets.'

The skinny man snickered. 'You betcha, Lafe.' He dismounted quickly, joined by the boy. The blonde girl noted that as the youngster took the money from them he did so with a shamefaced look. But the other man wrenched watches from pockets and

9

rings from fingers with a disdain for the owners.

The big one called Lafe watched them, grinning. When they walked back with the valuables they had taken from the passengers he grinned even more widely. He nodded at the women. He said suggestively, 'Now, it ain't real neighbourly not to offer these ladies a little attention.' He looked the women over with a leer. He jerked his head towards an outcrop of rocks a little distance from the coach.

'That looks like a nice friendly little spot. Ain't the red velvet of a cat house but good an' private.' He ran his eyes over the three women again. He said, 'You an' me, Chuck, let's you an' me take a couple of the ladies over there an' git to know 'em a little better.'

He stared at the two overly made-up girls. 'Git over there, you two.' The two women, a little apprehensive but used to rough handling from miners and cowhands and town layabouts, moved off wearily, the man called Chuck holding a pistol on them and herding them towards the rocks, a lascivious, vacuous grin on his face.

The big man swung down off his horse. He jerked out at the boy, 'Stay here an' keep an eye on these travellers, kid. You ain't ready for this kind of action yet.' As he turned to follow Chuck and the other women he threw a glance at the blonde. He said thickly, 'We'll come back for you later, goldie. Reckon it'll take two of us to handle you.'

As he left, the youngster stood facing the group with his pistol fixed on them. The blonde girl could see that although he did not like what was taking place he was trying to accept it as part of his apprenticeship.

Suddenly there was a scream from behind the rocks, followed by another one. The blonde glared at the five other men. 'Aren't any of you gentlemen going to make a move?'

The men shifted their feet uncomfortably. The shotgun guard switched the chaw in his mouth from one side to the other. He muttered, 'That big *hombre* is Lafe Larsen. He is one real bad man. Kill a man quicker than shoot a jack rabbit.'

The blonde shook her head angrily, eyes blazing. There was the sound of hoofbeats, a horse walking. A rider came up over the rise the coach had just driven up before it was halted.

He was a tall man, as lean as a rail, leathery-skinned, but sitting his horse, a giant black with a white blaze and four white socks, with the ease of a tough, saddle-hardened rider. A man perhaps in the mid-thirties, his face was cut out of rock, sharply-etched, the bones clean and hard, with eyes that were as blue and bright as the sky on a clear winter's day.

He was clean-shaven, a daily practice it seemed, and his vest, shirt and levis were neat and tidy. A holstered Smith & Wesson .44 sat on his right hip. He pulled up his horse, looking calmly at the boy who, startled, had swung the gun he held to point it at the newcomer.

The man on the big horse drawled softly, 'Now, that is not a friendly gesture, son. I'd admire if you would point that weapon in another direction.' The boy stared at him, not quite sure what to say or do.

There was movement from behind the rocks and the two men called Lafe and Chuck came back into view. The women staggered out from behind them, their clothes ripped and torn. One woman, sobbing, was cursing the two men in a high-pitched voice. The other seemed to be in shock.

The big hairy man spotted the rider. Scowling, he made his way quickly towards the coach, the other man following him fast.

Reaching the coach the man called Lafe Larsen glared up at the lean rider. He snarled, 'Keep ridin', stranger. Jest keep ridin', that's all.' The lean man stared back at him, the blue eyes clear and direct. He said mildly, 'Quite a little party you're having here.'

Larsen growled, 'But you ain't invited. Jest keep ridin', that's all.'

The stranger rested his left hand casually on the horn of his saddle. 'What if I say I'm too interested in what's going on here to leave?'

The man called Chuck had joined Larsen. He showed dirty teeth in a grimace of a grin. 'This feller oughta be showed a lesson, huh, Lafe?'

Larsen snarled, 'Shut up, I'll handle this.' His gross body dropped into a crouch. His voice became a gruff whisper. 'You high-tailin' it outa here, stranger?'

The lean rider shook his head. He said softly, 'No.' He kept his gaze fixed on the other man, staring right through him with eyes that burned in their sockets like twin blue flames. Larsen shook his head suddenly like a bemused bull, as if he wanted to shake off something that restrained and at the same time put a touch of uncertain fear into him.

His hand streaked for his gun but there was a momentary unsteady fumble before his fingers closed around the butt. His gun, clear of the holster, was first to roar but the shot went wide of the man in the saddle.

The gun was in the hand of the lean, blue-eyed man, steady as a rock. It thundered twice. Larsen's legs began to go from beneath him as if a great weight had fallen on him from above. There were two sudden holes in his chest which blood began to pour through like water from a rusty tank. He fell and lay still, his gross face become an instant death mask.

The man called Chuck was plucking frantically at his own weapon. He fired wildly at the lean man. The stranger's gun again bucked in his hand. Chuck spun around like a roulette wheel, the gun falling from his paralysed grasp. He fell alongside Larsen, a twin corpse.

The shotgun guard licked his lips. He croaked, 'Second-shot Sullivan... He let 'em both draw first an' then he nailed each of 'em.'

The passengers were staring, still shaking at the chilling fury of the encounter. The

14

man called Sullivan looked quietly at the youth standing there, his gun dangling helplessly from his shocked hand. Sullivan said offhandedly, 'Drop that gun or you'll join these two.'

The youth, quivering a little, let his pistol fall to the ground. Sullivan went on tonelessly, 'Now, hit the trail.' The boy stumbled towards his horse. Sullivan said curtly, 'Leave the horse be. You're going on foot. Back the way you came.'

The boy swung around to stare at him. 'You ain't – you can't let me...' He waved his arm. 'There ain't nothing out there. It's dead man's country.'

Sullivan nodded. 'Like your two friends here. And if you don't start stepping it out you're going to join them right now. The law is real hard on stage robbers.'

The youth threw him a wild look but the blue eyes pierced him with their frightening gaze. He gave one last pleading look but the lean rider merely jerked the gun in the direction he had told the youth to go.

The youngster took off, his gait unsteady, heading across the stony, open tract from which the three hold-up men had come.

The blonde girl spoke up, the only one who did not seem shaken by what had happened. 'You're not going to let that boy go out there on foot alone? No horse, no canteen, no nothing.'

Sullivan turned his gaze towards her. 'Yes, ma'am, I am.'

'But he's so young.'

'Young hold-up men can turn into old outlaws, ma'am. His mistake was riding with the wrong company. If he survives maybe he'll choose better companions.'

He looked over at the shotgun guard. 'Oldtimer, round up the horses these crow-bait were riding and hitch them up to the back of the stage. Guess they were all stolen, anyway.'

The guard moved quickly to do what he was told. Sullivan looked towards the two women who had been attacked. They had reached the coach now, staring dumbly at the dead men who just minutes before had been assaulting them.

Sullivan ran his eyes over the two dishevelled figures, his gaze suddenly taking on a look of disdain. 'Saloon girls, huh? Well, I hope the men in Estrada don't treat you quite as rough as these two.'

The blonde, giving him a cold stare, went past him to help the other two women back into the stage coach, calling them by name.

16

Sullivan, who had formerly treated her with some respect, narrowed his eyes. He said softly, 'Another saloon girl. Maybe I shouldn't have bothered.'

The blonde, hearing him, twisted her head to glare at him, her handsome face reddening. 'You kill two men in cold blood, send a boy out on foot to maybe his death and you still have the gall to look down on us as if we were dirt.'

Sullivan closed his eyes down to narrow slits of blue fire. 'The two I shot were nogoods, better out of the way. You know that. And that kid might not die. If he doesn't he'll know better next time. And I have never felt myself called on to show respect to saloon girls.'

The driver moved to climb back on to his seat. Sullivan swung down off his horse. He called to the guard, 'Come and help me with these two.' He strode over to the dead men. Between them they lifted the bodies of the two hold-up men and slung them over their mounts, the horses moving skittishly at the smell of blood and the limp weights.

The passengers had got back in, the blonde girl helping the other two women into their seats, one of them still sobbing brokenly. Sullivan watched them impassively. He nodded up at the driver, who shook the reins and moved the team off, Sullivan trotting alongside on the big black horse.

The shotgun guard looked across at the lean rider. He breathed to the driver, 'Yeah, that's him OK. Second-shot Sullivan.'

The driver gaped. 'You ain't kiddin'?'

The guard shook his head. 'Nope. Sure as shootin', that's him.' His eyes held an excited gleam. 'Did yuh see how he looked at them two afore they pulled a gun on him? It's them eyes of his. They sorta make a man facin' him lose his nerve. They shoot first an' they shoot wild. An' then he plugs 'em. Yes, sir, he plugs 'em.' He grinned happily. 'Estrada's gunna have *some* lawman. He's tamed more towns than Wild Bill Hickok.'

The driver stared. 'You mean he's gunna be our marshal?'

The guard nodded. 'Sure. I heerd that Judge Archer was gunna invite him to come and that's sure enough what he's done.'

Later they drove on into the town. Estrada was a flourishing place, set in rich cow country, one of the prime towns in cattle-raising California. Sullivan from the back of the big black horse looked down the main street as they drew up in front of the stage depot. He could see a number of saloons

18

and numerous stores. If people remained peaceable this was going to be a good place to live.

He rubbed his strong, lean jaw thoughtfully. Trouble was, if things kept happening like they had on his first contact with Estrada he was going to be kept busier than he had ever been. He hoped it wasn't going to pan out that way.

A crowd was gathering, already buzzing with excitement at the sight of the two bodies of the hold-up men slung over the horses. Among them was a short, round barrel of a man with a big moustache who despite his paunch and stubby legs had an air of command about him. He pushed through the crowd to the man on the big black horse. 'Martin Sullivan – welcome!'

The lean rider reached down and took the chubby hand stretched up to him. 'Good to see you, Judge.'

The judge rapped, 'Thought you'd come on the stage.'

Sullivan patted the neck of his horse. 'No. Figured I'd ride Ace all the way. I was just behind your stage when it left Willow Creek and I tagged along a mile or so back, not hurrying. Just as well I did.'

The judge nodded at the bodies on the

19

horses. 'Your work?'

'Afraid so, Judge.'

The little man nodded satisfiedly. 'Unless I miss my guess one of them is Lafe Larsen. He's been a thorn in our sides for quite a while. You've made a big impression on the local folks, Martin. But you'll want to get your horse to the livery. I've got a buggy waiting and I'll take you round to our place when you're ready.'

Sullivan nodded and kneed Ace on. As he did so he caught a glimpse of the blonde girl getting out of the stage. She gave him a look of utter hostility. As he rode on he thought, the feeling is mutual, lady. He hoped she didn't pack a hide gun. He didn't fancy getting plugged in the back by a derringer in the hand of a malicious saloon girl.

Ace moved on, neighing, the anticipated smell of grain and water in his nostrils.

TWO

Martin Sullivan walked around the office and the adjoining cells, inspecting his new centre of law and order.

He noted that it was well equipped with desk and chairs, an excellent array of guns in a rack on the wall, the cells strong and evidently prisoner-proof. It looked, he thought, a very good stronghold from which to keep off a mob that might want to lynch a prisoner.

He gave it one all-sweeping glance. Yes, he had been placed nicely. All he had to do now was see the law was kept. He hoped that was not going to be too difficult in the town of Estrada.

The front door was pushed open and a man walked in. He was about medium height with a square-cut build. He wore a moustache that was beginning to show a good deal of grey and there were deep lines around his mouth and eyes.

Sullivan looked particularly at the man's eyes. He always used them as a barometer of a human being's personality. These eyes, grey and a little faded, gave him a certain feeling of caution about the man.

The newcomer spoke, putting out his hand. 'Guess you're Sullivan. I'm Jim Moran, your deputy. A lotta people call me Legs.'

Sullivan took the other man's hand, shook it and released it. He enquired, 'Legs? Any special reason for that?'

Moran licked his lips, a little hesitant. 'Well, ain't no real cause 'cept that maybe when I have a few drinks I kinda walk a mite funny.'

Sullivan gave him a hard look. 'That happen often?'

Moran licked his lips again, his eyes not quite meeting those of the new marshal. 'Well, no more than ordinary with most men, I guess.'

Sullivan's look grew harder. 'We are not ordinary men. We are upholders of the law. We don't send out drunks to arrest other drunks. If we are going to uphold the law we have to have standards. You savvy?' Moran was silent.

Sullivan commented, 'Your given name is Jim. That's what I'll call you. I don't like that other name they've tagged you with. It doesn't sit too well on an officer of the law.'

Moran was quiet. Sullivan said briskly, 'Well, I guess we'd better have a drink and talk a little.' The other man stared, surprised. Sullivan grinned, something that one imagined he did not do too often. When he did the ice in his blue eyes broke up and there was warmth there. He pointed to the pot-bellied stove in the middle of the room. 'Coffee's what I mean.'

Moran, trying to hide a touch of disappointment, went to the stove to light it up. He put a handful of beans in the pot and pushed it on top of the stove. He gave Sullivan a flickering glance. 'You sure handled them two stage robbers. Lafe Larsen been givin' us a lotta trouble. A real bad man.'

Sullivan's voice was caustic. 'There is no bad man that can buck the law when it is properly applied. Why didn't your previous marshal apply it?'

Moran paused at the stove. A faint look of disgust passed quickly across his face. 'Didn't put on enough pressure, I guess. Maybe that's been a problem gin'rally wi' the law here lately.'

Sullivan said, 'Well, we're here to change that. I guess I'll have your unqualified support – even when lead might be flying.'

Moran turned back to the stove. He said

irritably, 'Don't worry, Marshal. Lead don't scare me.' Sullivan, staring at the other man's back, wondered what *did* scare him. Maybe it was liquor.

They were sitting at the desk, sipping at their mugs of hot coffee, when the door opened again. A figure walked in. It was covered with dust and its lips were cracked and the eyes still red-rimmed from walking in open desert country in a blazing sun. The figure walked a little unsteadily to a vacant chair and sat down.

Sullivan's eyes narrowed to the same slits they had become in the shoot-out at the stage coach. He said, his voice cold and hard, 'You're the kid who was with those two I turned into stiffs yesterday.'

The boy nodded with an effort. 'Yeah, I wandered around a while but figured there was really only one place to go – here in Estrada. Went to an eating-house and got me some coffee. Sure tasted good. They told me there about the new marshal.'

Sullivan kept his blue eyes boring into those of the youth. 'So?' The boy stared straight back at him. All the road agent pretence was gone and the marshal found himself looking at a repentant, fundamentally honest and decent boy.

24

'Well, I came to you because you know about me and I guessed I oughta sort of give myself up.'

Sullivan took another sip at his coffee. Moran was listening interestedly. Sullivan said, 'Well, I guess your doing that has delivered us all from the dangerous activities of a wild desperado.'

The boy offered pleadingly, 'Name's Jerry Owens. Came off a homesteader's farm. A very poor living. Struggling all the time. Figured it would be one less mouth for my pa to feed. Met up with those two fellers in a town near our place.' He gulped. 'They sorta convinced me that if you want something in this world you oughta take it. Real sorry I went along with them. They sure turned out to be real nasty men.'

Sullivan passed a contemplative finger across his steel-hard jaw. 'Well, now you've given yourself up like a murdering law-breaker we've got to decide what to do with you.'

He looked at Moran. The deputy was grinning. He said promptly, 'Set him to cleanin' out the jailhouse.'

The marshal grunted, 'That's really your job.' He looked across at the boy. 'You can bunk in the jailhouse and eat with us until we can figure out some way to clean that wholesale robbery and slaughter off your hands. That suit you?'

The boy nodded eagerly, something in his eyes indicating that he had found a real-life hero in this marshal that had entirely replaced the two who had so utterly disillusioned him. 'Yes, sir. That's really good of you. It's fine. I'll do whatever you say.'

Sullivan indicated a broom. 'Get yourself on the end of that and sweep this place out – cells and all. Like I said, it's really the job of Jim here but he'll just stay here and make sure you do it real well.'

The boy jumped to his feet and grabbed the broom. 'Yes, sir. Thank you, sir. I sure am glad you're doing this for me.'

Sullivan said drily, 'Isn't every day I get the chance to convert a hardened criminal.' He looked at Moran. 'Watch him. Jim. I think I'll take a stroll around the saloons and see if there's any crooked wheels or rotgut not really fit to drink.'

He went out on to the boardwalk and set off down the main street. He had visited several saloons when he drew level with one that had every sign of prosperity. There was a blazing, beautifully painted sign over the front that told all and sundry it was the

Bonne Chance saloon.

Sullivan mused, 'H'm, a big Frog in the local pond. Wonder how much good luck his patrons really have?' He went in. The bar was ornate, a gaudy, gilt affair with huge mirrors and a mile-long painting of a near-naked, reclining woman. The brass footrail glittered like gold. The chairs and tables were all in good order, not broken and scuffed like many others in similar places. The Frenchman evidently kept good order in his tavern.

Sullivan looked around for the owner. He didn't have far to look. A man was sauntering around the saloon, evidently checking on everything before business really took over later in the day.

Sullivan surveyed him carefully. The man was tallish, sinewy and moved with a lithe grace. He was dressed in a smart frock coat, silken, brocaded vest and striped trousers obviously the product of some smart big-city tailor. His shoes shone with polish and a silken handkerchief peeped from a top pocket in his coat while a boutonnière gleamed in his lapel.

The man wore his hair in a swept-back pompadour, black and shining with some scented lotion. He had typical sharp Gallic features and a thin, carefully tended moustache decked his upper lip. He looked a languid dandy but Sullivan saw deeper. There was a steely muscularity beneath all the fancy trappings and Sullivan instinctively knew that this was a man who could handle a Bowie knife like the famous colonel himself. No doubt also he would have a derringer planted on his body somewhere in the manner of the type of experienced saloon-keeper he was. Sullivan walked up to him. The man looked at him, eyebrow raised enquiringly.

Sullivan said, 'Martin Sullivan, the new marshal in town. Judge Archer was in touch with me on behalf of the townsfolk about taking over from your last peace officer.'

The Frenchman's eyes gleamed a little. 'Ah, *m'sieur*, you have already impressed the community. Lafe Larsen had become entirely too troublesome.' He put out a well-manicured hand. 'Eugene Latour, at your service.'

Sullivan shook the hand offered him. 'You are a long way from New Orleans, *m'sieur*.'

Latour smiled. 'Indeed. But I did not flee that beautiful city for any – ah – questionable reason. Not even because of killing a man in a duel over some lovely *mam'selle*.

Although I must admit I may have done so if called upon to. I have what you Americans call an eye for the ladies.'

Sullivan ran another glance over him. 'And I don't doubt quite a few ladies have had an eye for you.'

The Frenchman bowed, still smiling. *'Certainement, m'sieur.* I have had my share of affairs of the heart.'

There was a rustling of feminine skirts and Sullivan swung his head around. A blonde girl was approaching them, looking stunning in a silken gown, her hair done up in charming golden ringlets. She wore high-heeled shoes of soft kid leather and there was a sparkling necklace at her throat.

Latour turned to meet her. 'Here is living evidence of my – ah partiality for the opposite sex, Marshal. This is a young lady I have brought all the way from Kansas to further adorn my – ah – palace of good luck.' He gestured. 'She is Miss Lilian Blainey, otherwise known as The Kansas Sunflower.'

Sullivan stared at the blonde girl he had seen on the stage coach. She said coldly, 'We have already met, Eugene. I am sure Estrada is now in strong hands. One might almost say perhaps a little too strong.'

Sullivan asked abruptly, 'How are those

29

two girls?'

Her eyes flashed. 'One is coming out of shock, the other one is more used to man-handling and she will soon have recovered. But you scarcely showed all that concern yesterday, Marshal.'

He said bluntly, 'Saloon girls are not exactly in the business of discouraging male advances, ma'am.'

The girl said heatedly, 'There is a vast difference between advances and assaults, Marshal.'

Sullivan shrugged. 'Maybe.' He looked back at the Frenchman. He said easily, 'I don't take you for a four-flusher, Latour, but I would like to look at your gambling equipment. Cowhands earn their money too hard to be cheated out of it.'

The Frenchman spread out open palms. 'But, of course, of course. It is your duty to see the games are run honestly. I will take you around, *m'sieur.'* He turned to the girl. 'I will see you later, *mam'selle.* We will talk then about the entertainment in the matter of song that you will provide. You will excuse us.'

As he walked away with the Frenchman, Sullivan could feel the blonde's eyes boring into his back. He was glad they were not the actual daggers she probably wished they were.

So, she was essentially an entertainer and not a woman of more dubious activity. But still a saloon girl and he considered them to be a tribe of the lowest order.

Later he went back to the jailhouse. It looked as neat and clean as if Sadie Torrence had been attacking it. Moran grinned at him. 'That kid's a dab hand with a broom. His ma must have taught him well.'

Jerry Owens spoke up. 'My ma was a hard-working lady. Us older kids always helped her out with the house chores.'

Sullivan said, 'I like a man who admires his mother. You'd have done better to have stayed at home and kept on showing your admiration.'

The boy said definitely, 'Too many mouths to feed, like I said. They're all better off back there with me out fendin' for myself.'

'Trouble is,' asked the marshal, 'how do you figure you are going to keep fending for yourself?'

The boy's face lit up. 'How about making me your deputy?'

Sullivan's eyebrows rose. 'I've already got a deputy.'

The boy was enthusiastic. 'Yeah, I know.

31

But nothing like having two. Jim Moran might get blown apart by some badman gunnie.'

Moran said sourly, 'Thanks, kid. But that gunnie might git you before he gits me.'

Jerry Owens said stoutly, 'Well, maybe, but leastways I would have died defendin' the law.'

Sullivan hid a grin. 'We'll figure out something to do with you. Meantime I've got to find some lodgings. Judge Archer tells me Sadie Torrence runs a good place.'

Moran nodded. 'None better. She is one fine lady.' He mumbled, 'Had notions of marryin' that widow but...' His voice tailed off.

Sullivan said shortly, 'I maybe gather she didn't want to marry a drinking man.' Moran was silent.

The marshal said, 'I'll go see her. I don't really fancy the chow I prepare.'

Sadie Torrence was a buxom lady with big motherly breasts, hair tied back in a business-like way and eyes that looked at everyone as direct and openly as only a thoroughly honest person could. After they had agreed on terms she asked curiously, 'Why didn't you check in at a saloon, maybe like the Bonne Chance? Plenty of liquor handy.'

Sullivan nodded. 'And plenty of saloon girls, too. I don't have much liking for either.'

She bristled. 'What have you got against saloon girls? I was one once before I got married. I ain't too proud of some of the things I did but I never robbed a man at any time ever.' She grew more voluble. 'Out here in the west a lotta girls are forced into it. Either that or starve to death somewhere.' She gave him a keen look. 'I'll bet that you bein' a bachelor did not absolutely pass every one of them by.'

Sullivan admitted, 'Well, there have been times when I...' He concluded doggedly, 'But that's all they're good for.'

Sadie Torrence snorted, 'Ain't that jest like a man? Take the comfort he can find in a woman's arms an' then go around black-guardin' them.'

Sullivan winced a little. He could see Sadie Torrence was a straight talker and maybe he was going to suffer a little at her hands. But when he thought of the meal she had prepared for him and the others that night he guessed he would just have to grin and bear it. He grinned right there and then. This sure was a feisty lady.

THREE

Judge Achilles Archer stood in the centre of the marshal's office and looked about him. He glanced at the five-pointed star on Sullivan's chest and he smiled.

'Good to see that badge sitting there. We have a real lawman at last.'

Sullivan shrugged. 'Just a town marshal, Judge, not a Federal lawman, not a US marshal appointed by the president. Not even a sheriff with control of a county.' The judge patted him on the shoulder. 'Your turn will come, Martin. You are a first-class peace officer. One day your jurisdiction will extend over an entire territory.'

'Better hurry up, Judge. I am not getting any younger.'

'Nonsense, man. You've got years ahead of you. What are you? Thirty-five? Six?'

Sullivan nodded. 'A couple of months off the latter. And, I tell you, Judge, I am starting to feel it.' He grimaced. 'Must have been all those years trail driving and herding cows.' He started to hum a little song. 'Oh, say, little dogie, when will you lie down, and give up this shifting and roving around? My horse is leg weary, and I'm awfully tired. But if you get away I'm sure to get fired...'

His eyes had a faraway, reminiscent look. He murmured, 'You know, Judge, on one of those drives we had the herd stampede ten times in one night. I got thrown off my pony and went under their hoofs. Laid up for weeks.'

The judge said quietly, 'Tough times but they're behind you now. No need to be scared of any more stampedes.'

Sullivan said drily, 'No – only of a bullet in the back. Or even in the front from someone faster than me.'

The judge snapped, 'Stuff and nonsense. You can handle anything that comes along.' He paused a moment. 'Although I must say that habit of yours of letting the other man shoot first would not be much to my liking.'

Sullivan's eyes held a touch of quiet humour with a firm confidence behind it. 'Upsets 'em, Judge. They see I am not hurrying and it makes 'em try to be even a little faster. Spoils the aim. You know, it's like an old gunnie said, it's not really the speed that counts, it's the accuracy.'

The judge shook his head. 'Not a philosophy I'd care to adopt in a gun fight but I guess you know what you're doing.' He looked keenly at the lawman. 'You know, Martin, you ought to be married.'

Sullivan asked lightly, 'You got someone in mind for me, Judge?'

The little barrel of a man said slowly, 'I have a daughter called Faith. She is seventeen years old and although I say it myself she is one spanking looker.' He surveyed the marshal and shook his head. 'If only you had eight years less on you, Martin, and if you were not–'

Sullivan offered, 'Such a case-hardened rover?' He smiled, the icy-blue eyes dissolving into warmth. 'Save your daughter for some young buck with more ahead of him than maybe a grave on Boot Hill.'

A buckboard pulled up across the street. It was driven by a youngish man with blond hair and the look of an accomplished cowman. Even sitting on the seat of the buckboard it could be seen that he was tall and hard muscled, a man to throw a cow and have it branded before it had time to twitch its tail.

Beside him was a woman in a divided skirt with elegant knee-high boots of soft leather. She wore a fancy, colourful shirt and a white stetson. As she stood up and stepped down to the ground she took off her hat and used it to flap some trail dust from off her clothes. When she did so her hair came into view, black and lustrous as an Indian squaw's, hanging down her back in one long, shining, plaited tail. She looked momentarily across the other side of the street.

Even at that distance it could be seen that her eyes were pools of brown beauty and her lips as red and moist as wine in a glass. As she walked away from the buckboard her hips and body moved with the grace of a dancer.

The judge caught Sullivan staring at her with tense open admiration. The judge nodded. 'Yes, a beauty, isn't she?' He went on briskly. 'The widow of Curly Cavendish, boss of the Slash C, biggest outfit in this part of the state. Curly went to 'Frisco once and came back with her. I understand she was some sort of an entertainer in some show place or other. From the moment he saw her I guess she had Curly roped and tied.'

He looked thoughtfully across the street at the woman who was disappearing into a store, her driver waiting for her outside. He went on. 'Damn near busted Curly. Had him spending money on her like it was water from a spring that was never going to run dry. Fancy furniture, a grand piano for her to play while she sings.'

He added, 'Big expensive trips to big towns.' His face grew morbid. 'Curly, I guess, was sort of love blind. But even he started to worry about how the money was going. He began to get loans on his property and finally ran into debt. Then one night he just went off on what seemed to have been a mad ride. Finished up, his horse fell and threw him. Curly broke his neck.'

He added slowly, 'Some say Curly's crazy act was also due to the fact that Theodora – that's her name – had switched her affections to that big hulk you see sitting on the buckboard. That's Ben Carson, foreman of the Slash C. Don't know about that, how true it might be.'

He kept gazing across the street. 'Yes, sir, that's Theodora Cavendish. She's a real beauty right enough but one is not sure whether or not it is in the line of Jezebel.' He sighed. 'Don't believe the Slash C has picked up much since Curly died. Near enough to real broke right now is my guess.'

He trailed off. 'Well, that's the story of Theodora and Curly Cavendish and the Slash C – right up till now, that is.' He added thoughtfully, 'Unless, of course, Theodora has something else up her sleeve.'

He made for the door and stood there a moment. 'That what I was saying about taking a bride, Martin... Theodora Cavendish, I feel, would bring with her to any man a dowry of bad luck.' He stepped out the door.

Sullivan kept looking across the Street. The woman had come out of the store now with a package under her arm. As she handed it up to the man in the buckboard the marshal caught sight of her features again. They were dark, sultry, brooding. It was the face of an enchantress. Sullivan felt something moving inside him no saloon girl had ever stirred there.

He watched her as she said something to the man in the buckboard in a sharp, imperious manner. The man nodded quickly. Sullivan caught the look on the blond-haired foreman's face. It was that of a man wanting nothing but to please the woman. He thought, she's got him on a leash like a lap dog. The woman moved off to another store. Sullivan smiled. Probably to buy something for her personal adornment while the man waited patiently for her.

Jerry Owens suddenly came in. His young face was full of hope. 'Marshal, you gunna take me up on that deputy idea?'

Sullivan looked at him curiously. 'Where did you learn to say deputy instead of depitty?'

The boy said proudly, 'My ma taught us all our letters and more. She was a school marm before she married my pa.'

Sullivan inclined his head. 'A fine lady.' The boy nodded appreciatively. The marshal went on, 'Tell you what I'm going to do. I'm going to make you a deputy on certain conditions.'

The boy beamed. 'No matter what it is, I'll do it.'

Sullivan said carefully, 'Don't look for trouble. Watch me and do everything I do and' – his smile again broke the ice of his eyes – 'stay away from the saloon women and find yourself an honest girl. I've been without one long enough to know what they can mean to a man.'

The boy whooped, 'Yip-ee! Now I can write home and tell my folks I'm a real live lawman.'

Sullivan said drily, 'That might not please them all that much – especially your ma. I think she might have had more peaceable things in mind.'

Jerry Owens went to speak but Sullivan

stopped him. 'Tonight I'm going to take you on a round of the saloons with me. Just watch everything I do. Our aim is to stop trouble wherever it starts but never to go looking for it.' He went to a drawer and took out a tin star and pinned it on the boy.

Jerry Owens looked at it admiringly. Sullivan said, 'One day, being lucky and dodging bullets, you might wear a gold badge that sometimes sheriffs get instead of a tin one. But whether it's tin or gold, honour it just the same.'

The boy nodded solemnly. Sullivan thought, now I've got to be nursemaid to a kid. But somehow the thought with this boy was not unpleasant.

It was when they went into the Bonne Chance that night that Sullivan saw the woman again.

She was dressed differently this time. Her lustrous black hair was piled on top of her head in shining coils. She wore an expensive silken gown with a provocative view of firm, shapely breasts, a pearl pendant nestling between them.

She had evidently stayed in town for the night. She was sitting at a table with the elegant Eugene Latour. There was no sign of the blond foreman. Sullivan thought, he's probably in another saloon drinking himself into a mood of green-eyed jealousy.

He looked at Latour. No money maybe at the Slash C but plenty of it in Latour's pocket and it looked like he was spending some of it on Theodora Cavendish. He directed his gaze back at the woman. No doubt of it – she would take away the breath of Casanova himself. Jerry Owens alongside him whistled softly. 'Boy, that sure is some lady.'

Sullivan said curtly, 'We are not here to admire the women-flesh, boy.'

The youngster, chastened, nodded. 'Right, Marshal, right.'

The sound of gunshots from outside split the air. A wild yell accompanied the sound followed by more shots. Sullivan made for the door, the boy at his heels.

Out in the street a figure was whirling around, pistol in hand. He was letting off the shots and whooping at the same time. He had come out of a saloon and had already smashed out a light in front of the place with one shot. Inside the saloon he had left there was a scurrying for cover.

The man with the gun bawled, 'Git down on the floor, you mangy cowhands an' stay down – I aim to blow a hole in the first man that stands up.'

The boy gasped, 'Why, that's – that's Jim Moran.'

Sullivan rasped, 'Legs Moran, more like. He's all likkered up and walking like a drunken sailor.' He bit out, 'He was supposed to be patrolling the other end of the town. Instead he's been in there taking on a bellyful of happy juice. Well, he's got some unhappy moments coming.'

He walked out into the street towards the raging man. He called softly, 'Moran, look this way. I'm the marshal and I'm telling you to put down that weapon.'

Moran spun around drunkenly. 'Hey, what's that – what you buttin' in for?'

Sullivan kept walking towards him. 'Put the gun down and hold out your hands. I'm putting the cuffs on you and taking you down to the jailhouse.'

Moran, brain befuddled but in an ugly and dangerous mood, roared, 'No one's arrestin' me. I do the arrestin' around here. Jest stay right where you are or I'll blast you in your tracks.' He pointed the gun at Sullivan, drink-inspired rage convulsing at his face.

The marshal suddenly bent down and

picked up a stone. He hurled it with a lightning throw at the drunken deputy. It hit Moran's gunhand with a cracking sound and the pistol flew from his grasp. Howling with frustration, the deputy scrambled after the gun.

But Sullivan had reached him now and the toe of the marshal's boot was thudding into the deputy's head with a sound like an axe driven with force into wood. Moran grunted and lay still.

The marshal bent down and in one heaving moment lifted the unconscious deputy, slinging him across his back. A group had piled out of the Bonne Chance to watch.

As Sullivan, carrying the slack weight of the deputy, went past them he caught a glimpse of Latour and Theodora Cavendish. The black-haired woman was staring at him with a look of strongly aroused interest. She was smiling as she stared straight into the face of the marshal. She was clapping gloved hands together in applause.

Sullivan felt the same stirring again as his eyes met hers. There was a flash of responsive fire there that told him she was a woman who liked brute force. He wondered if he was going to know her better.

When they got back to the jailhouse Jerry

Owens went ahead and opened the door for him. Sullivan dropped the untidy bulk that was Jim 'Legs' Moran on the floor. He barked at the boy, 'Get me a pail of water.' The boy stared and then moved quickly to obey. When he came back Moran was groaning and starting to move, his body struggling to get up.

Sullivan waited until he got to his knees and then grabbed the deputy in a grip of steel and forced his head down into the pail of water.

Moran's arms and legs flailed helplessly. Sullivan jerked his head out of the water and then as the deputy spluttered for breath jammed it down into the water again.

Again Moran's body went through the thrashing motions. Sullivan pulled his head out again. The deputy's face was turning blue.

The marshal rammed his head into the water once more and held it down longer this time. When the deputy's movements grew weaker and almost stopped the marshal jerked his head out again and let him collapse on the floor.

Sullivan jerked a chair towards him with one foot and sat down on it. The boy standing nearby shivered just a little as he took a peek at the marshal's face. It was like that of a judge facing a prisoner on whom he was about to deliver a savage sentence.

Moran finally floundered back into full consciousness. He sat up a little, blinking red-rimmed eyes at the marshal out of a blue, water-sodden face.

Sullivan bit out, 'Get this, Jim Moran, and get it good. If I find you drunk again, on or off duty, I will dunk your head in that pail and not take it out. I will not have a man around me who disgraces the star he wears.'

He motioned to the boy. 'Help him to a cell and let him sleep it off.' As the older man hobbled to a cell with the help of the boy he glared weakly at the marshal, deep resentment in his eyes.

When the boy came back Sullivan said harshly, 'That critter will need watching. He may try to get back at me. If he does, I'll kill him.'

He looked at the boy and his face relaxed. 'Get off to your lodgings, kid. We're through for the night.'

As the boy left the youngster was thinking, this is what my ma would call a no-nonsense man. In spades.

FOUR

Sullivan looked up from the desk as the deputy, Moran, came stumbling out of the cell, surly, disgruntled. He stopped beside the marshal. His voice was full of rancour.

'You had no call to handle me like that. That's the way you handle a street drunk.'

Sullivan eased himself back in his chair. 'Well, what else are you?'

Moran bridled. 'Maybe you want me to hand in my star.'

Sullivan said briefly, 'Not necessarily that. What I do want you to do is to start behaving like a true officer of the law.'

Moran mumbled, 'There's some guys in this town that think I'm a joke. When they start talking like that I don't like it.'

Sullivan corrected him. 'When you're drunk you don't like it. Stop getting drunk and they'll stop riding you.'

Moran muttered, 'You don't know what it's like to want a drink real bad.'

'No, I don't because I never took enough to make me want it like that.' He said flatly,

'But I'm telling you this. Get over your yen for it or get out.' He turned to the desk. 'But now there's business to do. I hear there's a little rustling been going on. Ned Munro, boss of the Flying M, put in a complaint yesterday about it. You know him?'

Moran nodded. He mumbled, 'Yeah, he's a good honest guy. Doesn't look for help unless he can't handle it himself. Must have tried.'

Sullivan agreed. 'That he has. But now he wants our help. Get out there and talk to him about it.'

Jim Moran hesitated. 'You handing it over to me?'

The marshal nodded. 'Yes. Why not?' He added coolly, 'Besides, there are no bar-rooms over that way.'

The deputy reddened a little. 'OK. I'll ride over and see Ned.'

As he left, Sullivan called, 'When you come back we'll talk over what you found out.'

Moran flipped a hand in reply. Sullivan watched him steadily as he left the office, heading for his horse. The deputy's back was straightening up a little already.

Jerry Owens, who had let Jim Moran out of the cell and tidied up after him, had heard all the conversation. He asked incredulously, 'You letting that soak still handle lawman business?'

Sullivan faced him. 'You've got a lot to learn, boy. That is the very best way of changing him from being a soak. Give him something to do that makes him responsible. From what I can gather your last marshal didn't give him enough to do, so Jim Moran spent a lot of his time hanging around the saloons and drinking too much. I'll work him till the boozy sweat runs out of him.'

Jerry Owens blinked. 'Hey, you might have something there.'

'I have. And now I want you to see the Widow Purvis. Someone stole her cat. She doesn't know who. Maybe it was someone who was tired of rats gnawing in their cellar. Or maybe it was a kid who wanted a pussy playmate. Anyway, go and talk to her about it.'

The boy shook his head disgustedly. 'The case of the missing kitty. Sweeping out this place, trying to find lost cats. When am I gunna get real lawman's stuff to do?'

Sullivan said, 'Maybe sooner than you think. It often happens that way.'

Later in the morning Jim Moran came back in. Sullivan, who had just finished some desk work, looked at him questioningly.

The deputy said gruffly, 'Ned Munro has had cows rustled a couple of times lately. Not many. Amounts to about seven or eight. Says he thinks it's maybe someone jest tryin' their hand, sorta aimin' for somethin' bigger later on. Hasn't been able so far to track down where they been driven to. All he knows is it's south – maybe even as far as the border.'

'Uh-huh. Well, we'll have to see if we can track 'em a little better.'

Moran changed the subject. He met the marshal's eyes. Sullivan could see that already he was starting to respond to having been trusted to do things. 'Took a walk around the town. The Palmers have ridden in – all four of 'em. Movin' from one saloon to another.'

'And who might the Palmers be?'

Moran clicked his tongue against his teeth. 'They are a bad family. Had a sorta head of the clan, a nasty old man who died a while back. Run a outfit, the Tumblin' P. Good name. It's tumblin' down to rack an' ruin. Some say they've done a little rustlin' here an' there. Word was that they robbed a bank one time over the border in Nevada. Anyway, there's these four brothers livin' out there together. They come to town now an' then an' when they do folks duck for cover.'

He stared hard at Sullivan. 'Our last marshal usually used ta be missin' when they was around. I tried tacklin' them alone once but they ganged up on me an' beat me up.'

Sullivan rested his chin on his hand. He said reflectively, 'We'll just have to watch what they get up to this time.' He asked, 'They are not acting up as yet, I take it?'

'No. But they are gettin' really tanked up. Tonight they are bound to be trouble.'

Sullivan nodded. 'Well, we'll cross that bridge when we come to it. Meantime you'd better just hang around in their general vicinity and keep your eye on them.' He added, 'That means, of course, that if you've got to drink it had better be sarsaparilla.'

Moran gave him a steady look. 'Yeah. Yeah. Sarsaparilla will be fine.'

It was in the evening when Sullivan was preparing to go on his walk around the town that Jim Moran came in, breathing a little hard. Sullivan noted that his mouth was twitching a trifle nervously.

The deputy burst out, 'Them Palmers. They are really actin' up in the Bonne Chance saloon. Looks like they are gunna take it over – girls an' all. Real ugly.'

Sullivan enquired easily, 'What about that Frenchman who runs the place, Latour? He doesn't look to me like a man easily scared.'

Moran ejaculated, 'He faced 'em up but one of 'em buffaloed him from behind. They got him sittin' up now but with a gun on him. He ain't got no real gunhands workin' for him, no one who could take on these guys.'

Sullivan went across and took a scattergun off the rack and loaded it. He turned back. He said easily to the deputy, 'You say they look like laying hands on the women?'

Moran nodded. 'Yeah. They's one a real good-lookin' blonde. They call her The Kansas Sunflower. Big Rube Palmer, the family leader, got his eyes on her.' There was a sudden gleam of admiration in his eyes. 'But she's got some grit, that one. Standin' him off like he is some mangy coyote. Which he is.'

Sullivan mused, 'Well, saloon girls are not a tribe I especially admire but I suppose they have a right to who they let lay hands on them.'

He looked tentatively at Jerry Owens. The boy was standing by them, trembling with eagerness. The marshal said slowly, 'I don't really figure this is a business for you, kid, but after all you will make it three of us to their four.' He nodded at the rack. 'Get yourself a shotgun.'

The boy grasped it eagerly. Sullivan said, 'Now, stay close to me and if lead starts to fly get behind me. I mean that, boy – right behind.' As they went out the door he added, 'And try not to shoot yourself with that thing.'

He stopped for a moment. 'Jim, keep an eye out for backshooters. If you see one, nail him.' The deputy nodded. He was walking now with no sign of the old Legs Moran.

When they got to the Bonne Chance there was not a great deal of noise. There was just some growling voices and then suddenly the smashing of a bottle. Jim Moran said in a low voice, 'That's probably Big Rube cracking the neck off a bottle agin the bar an' havin' a free drink.'

Sullivan said gently, 'Let's go in and see what's happening.'

Over against the bar one of the biggest men Sullivan had ever seen in his life stood there. He was like a grizzly bear with most of the hair stripped off except for where it showed as a tangled growth across his forearms in his rolled-up sleeves and at the neck above his flannel undershirt.

He had the face of an evil buccaneer and legs and arms that could have had him wrestling an elephant. He put down the bottle he had broken open and from which he had just taken a great swig. Although he had been drinking best part of the day he was not drunk.

He looked across at the three newcomers and ran the back of one great fist across his mouth. It looked then as if the fist had painted the vast ugliness of the grin that now appeared there. His voice was loud and whiskey-hoarse. 'Ah, the law. An' you got your popguns with you, too. But we got more fire-power than you boys.'

He nodded at three other figures. They were big, slouch-shouldered, unkempt, their hair long and untidy. Each had a gun in his hand and looked as if his dearest wish was that someone would step out of line so that they could send a slug tearing through his vitals.

'That there is Jesse, that one is Caleb and that teeny one – why, he ain't no more than six feet – he's the young'un, Sammy.' The customers sat around, silent, apprehensive, one man almost slobbering with fear.

The saloon girls had been herded to one

side, crouching back, looking like a pack of farmyard turkeys hunted into a corner by a man with an axe.

One girl stood slightly in front of the others, blonde, upright, unafraid, eyes blazing with anger. It was the one they called The Kansas Sunflower. Sullivan flicked a glance at her, grudgingly impressed. Big Rube waved a hand with fingers like a string of greasy sausages at the girls.

'We aim to have some fun with the girls later. Me, I got my eye on that one with the gold hair.' He leered with heavy sexual innuendo plain in his eyes. Then he waved his hand towards the bar. There were a dozen bottles of whiskey and brandy set up there by a cringing bartender. 'An' I guess we'll have some more fun with that, too.'

He looked at Eugene Latour, white-faced and quivering with repressed anger, seated at a table with the youngest Palmer smirking as he held a gun on him. Big Rube went on, 'The Frenchy here, he complained a little about our takin' over but we persuaded the mon-sewer to see it our way.'

He scratched his forehead with the end of the barrel of his pistol. 'But now you lawmen come bustin' in an' we got another irritation.' He sucked at his teeth. 'Now, the way I see it we could start blastin' at one another an' some of them purty girls might git hurt.' He grinned. 'But, me, I like my fee-males in one piece.'

He leered at Sullivan. 'I got me an idee, Marshal. Let's bring all this down to you an' me.' He ran his eyes over Sullivan with shrewd summing-up. 'What say you an' me have a little rassle? I figure you might have done some in your time.'

He smiled proudly. 'I ain't never been beat in a rasslin' match but here's your chance, Marshal. If you win, we pack an' leave. If we win, you leave or we start shootin' some of these here male citizens – includin' you. Awful lotta people likely to get hurt in a gunfight.'

Sullivan was silent. He asked suddenly, 'No holds barred?' Big Rube showed a mouthful of teeth that looked like those of a wolf that had just been feeding on carrion.

'Now, that's the kind of talk I like to hear, Marshal. No ifs, no buts, but takin' up the challenge instanter. Your pree-deecessor would not have done that. Ever time he heard we was around he made sure he wasn't.' A sadistic glitter shone in his eyes. 'No holds barred, Marshal, was exactly what I was plannin', whether you had it in mind or not.'

He looked at his brothers and then at Jim Moran and Jerry. 'No firin' while the contest is bein' waged.' He reholstered the gun he was holding, untied his gunbelt and dropped it and swaggered closer to Sullivan. As he moved the floorboards creaked under his immense weight. Sullivan figured quickly, six-foot-five and three hundred pounds.

The marshal handed his scattergun to Moran and untied and dropped the gunbelt holding his Smith & Wesson .44. He moved over closer to the bar. Big Rube leered, 'No good tryin' to crowd me, Marshal. But I'll come your way.'

He dropped into a crouch, a bear on its hindlegs, eyes flaring with total confidence, arms outstretched to crush this man and break his back.

Sullivan's hand streaked to the bar, grabbed a bottle and in a forked lightning movement smashed it over Big Rube's head.

The startled giant tried to blink the sudden racing stream of blood out of his eyes but as he did so Sullivan kicked him in the throat, the toe of his boot driving deep into the flesh.

As Big Rube grunted with pain, Sullivan grabbed another bottle and smashed it between the giant's eyes. Big Rube began to fall to his knees. As he did, Sullivan kicked him again, with delicate precision, on the point of the jaw. The fight was over.

Smarting with shock and rage, Jesse Palmer lifted his gun and fired at Sullivan. But a split second before he did Jim Moran carefully put a bullet across the back of the Palmer brother's gunhand. The big man howled with pain and dropped his gun, his shot having gone wild.

Sullivan stood upright. He spoke clearly so all could hear. 'Everyone heard what Big Rube said. What this Palmer family has to do now is pick up Rube and leave quietly. We are not arresting them but if they come in here again with this kind of intent they can expect a reception that could be just a mite warmer.'

A few other men had suddenly produced guns and even the formerly cringing bartender was holding a scattergun on the Palmers from across the bar. The three lurching brothers, silent snarls twisting their Neanderthal lips, gathered up the great limp weight of their stricken brother and headed for the swing doors.

Sullivan nodded at Jim Moran and Jerry Owens. The two followed the Palmers, shot-guns at the ready and backed up by a few other men, to see the Palmers on their way.

Suddenly Sullivan was aware that the blonde girl was alongside him. Her voice was still cold but she said, 'Thank you, Marshal. That was–' she swallowed a little on the word – 'gallant.'

Sullivan said bluntly, 'A lawman has to defend anyone – even saloon girls.' The girl turned aside, a sudden complete chill in her eyes.

Eugene Latour stepped across from the table. He bowed to the marshal. *'Magnifique, mon ami.* I have never seen a thing like that done better. In fact, I have never seen a thing like that done before.' He touched his head painfully. 'I would have done something but unfortunately–'

Sullivan said curtly, 'Never let a bushwhacker get behind you, *m'sieur.'* He headed for the doors. The Palmers were riding away down the street, one of the brothers supporting Big Rube in the saddle, the guns of the watchers still trained on them.

Jerry Owens' eyes were gleaming. 'You were just great in there, Marshal. You never put one foot wrong.' Sullivan wondered about that as he felt a slight twinge about what he had said to the blonde girl. But then he shook the thought from him. He said aloud, 'Come on, there's more of the town to patrol.'

As they walked off he was thinking, Estrada is not exactly as peaceable as I had hoped.

FIVE

Sadie Torrence, helped by the local girl she employed to share the burden of running her room and board hostelry, was gathering up the dishes after the men had eaten and were leaving the long table at which they were served.

She stopped the marshal on his way out. She said curtly, 'That was a good thing you did at the Bonne Chance. Them Palmers needed curbin'. That daddy of theirs never took his belt to their big bottoms soon enough nor often enough.'

Sullivan inclined his head. 'Maybe they learned a lesson. Maybe they didn't. We'll see.' He turned to move off. She stopped him again, a big strong woman with an open face and an unwavering gaze.

'But it warn't too nice what you said to

that gal.'

Sullivan stared. 'What girl?'

Sadie said, 'That one they call The Kansas Sunflower. But her proper name is Lilian – Lilian Blainey.'

Sullivan stood still. 'I know her name. What did I say to her?'

'You told her that unfortunately as a lawman you gotta defend even saloon girls.'

He fixed the woman with a hard stare. 'I never used the word "unfortunately".'

'You as good as did. Someone heard you and passed on to me what you said and it warn't nice. She's human, you know, an' these things hurt.'

Sullivan enquired, 'How human and hurt does she feel when she's rifling some drunken cowhand's pockets?'

Sadie flared up. 'I bet she doesn't do that. Neither did I and I was a saloon girl onct.' Sullivan raised his eyebrows. She burst out, 'You men – you don't know what it's like to be a woman on the frontier. There's precious few jobs unless you want to be a laundress washin' stacks of filthy miners' clothes. Or maybe a cook or a waitress servin' men who are always tryin' to lay their hands on you. An', let me tell you, they ain't too many jobs even like that offerin' out here. They soon git filled up. Next best is marryin' some farmer or rancher an' bein' a drudge to him. An' a lotta them bring their wives with 'em from the east or elsewhere.'

She went on doggedly, 'I don't know how many other women you got wrong, Marshal, but you sure got that one dead wrong. Latour got her as a entertainer an' that's all she is.'

Sullivan asked blandly, 'Well, she might be an angel with feathers as white as a swan but what about the rest of the girls?'

Sadie Torrence said heatedly, 'Ain't you got no idea how a girl's face an' figger is a pleasure for a man to look on after he's been starin' at cows' backsides all week long? You mighta seen a lotta life, Marshal, and I guess you have but you have been mighty blind to some sides of it.'

Sullivan walked away, thoughtfully. This lady had convictions and even when you didn't go along with them you found yourself listening and weighing up what she had said.

Down at the jailhouse he had sent Jim Moran and Jerry Owens out on different jobs. The boy had found the Widow Purvis's cat and got it back to her. Moran, he found, had pretty good connections all around the town and the neighbouring ranches and was being more and more accepted lately as a dependable lawman.

At the moment Moran was still following up the loss of Ned Munro's stock. Sullivan thought, he would also have to take a hand there.

There was the sound of a buckboard pulling up outside. Sullivan looked towards the door. After a moment or two a woman came in. Sullivan looked up and felt a sudden quick surge of interest. It was Theodora Cavendish.

She wore the divided skirt again and the high boots, a richly coloured shirt and, what would have seemed incongruous in another woman but not in her, a string of pearls about her throat. She took off her hat to disclose her mass of shining black hair.

She smiled. 'Marshal, I haven't met you but I'm glad to have the opportunity. I was in the Bonne Chance that night you brought Jim Moran to his senses and I also heard about what you did there when you tamed the Palmer boys. I admire you.'

Sullivan got to his feet. 'Ma'am, I appreciate that but I've got to tell you I had two good deputies backing me up when I went after the Palmers.'

She smiled more deeply. 'One a boy and the other a souse?'

Sullivan corrected her. 'A boy who is a good man in the making and a deputy who is learning that liquor and lawmen don't really mix.'

She nodded. 'So be it.' She adopted another posture in which her shapely breasts stood out against the thin cloth of her shirt and the splendid curve of her hips was accentuated. 'Marshal, I am Theodora Cavendish, as I guess you know, and I'd like to invite you to have a meal with me one evening out at my ranch.'

Sullivan asked blandly, 'Why should you take it for granted that I know who you are?'

There was a glimpse of tantalization in the eyes that looked, he suddenly thought, like those of one of those houris he had once read about in *The Arabian Nights*.

'Marshal, there is no male who ever came to this town who doesn't know who I am. And if they don't know, they ask.'

He smiled. 'You do not underrate yourself, ma'am.'

'Never have and never will. I am a realist about these things. And don't call me ma'am. It makes me feel like a schoolmarm or a storekeeper's wife. But about that invitation – you accept?'

Sullivan nodded. 'A pleasure.'

She turned to go. 'Well, until then, *adios.*' He watched her go back to the buckboard. The same blond-headed burly figure sat up there holding the reins. His face held a look of vicious jealousy as the woman left the marshal's office and stepped back up alongside him.

Sullivan thought idly, that *hombre* is burning up inside over this woman and the other men she associates with. One day he is going to lash out at at least one of them. I hope I'm facing him if he ever tries it on me.

Eugene Latour welcomed the woman into his office, an elegant affair of fine rugs on the floor, a heavy cedar desk, luxurious armchairs and excellent pictures on the walls, one an original Corot.

Theodora Cavendish looked around her with a sigh. 'I love this room. You know how to live, Eugene.'

Latour handed her a glass of champagne. 'Ah, *ma cherie*, one does one's best in a savage environment.'

She took a sip at the champagne and waved a hand about her. 'All this could be added to if our plan goes through.'

Latour nodded. *'Oui.'* He enquired sharply, 'You are sure of the reliability of this man?'

She gestured wearily. 'My dear Eugene, you know he made his spread available and it is right on the fringe of the Mexican border. As I told you, Rance Horton was a crooked gambler for years. I met him in 'Frisco years ago. He decided to buy that ranch with his winnings at the table but it didn't pay off too well. He's prepared to do anything that will bring him ready cash.'

Latour fingered his chin. 'Well, we have already committed ourselves by sending a few rustled cattle down to him.'

She said persuasively, 'Of course, we have. And waiting on the other side of the border are all those hungry Mexican revolutionaries. Rance Horton has already made the contact with that rebel leader, de la Huerta. And he is ready to receive as many rustled cattle as we can get to him.'

Latour mused, 'De la Huerta would have quite a number of troops to feed. There will need to be many more cows sent down.'

The black-haired woman agreed. 'Yes. It's got to be done on a big scale. And it can only be done once.' She shot a sharp glance at him. 'We'll need more men. What about the Palmers?'

Latour tapped a finger-nail against his teeth. 'Maybe. I have heard they have rustled before.'

'They have and they are the kind of men we need – those who don't care what they do as long as there are dollars in it.'

Latour murmured, 'Just as long as they don't get out of hand as they did in the Bonne Chance recently.'

Her face suddenly changed. It took on the harsh lines of a woman with unscrupulous designs who was determined to carry them out come hell or high water. She said coldly, 'We'll keep them in line, Eugene. As you know, I'm near penniless. I don't intend to stay that way.'

He offered suggestively, 'Perhaps you have been too big a spender, *cherie.*'

She gave him a sudden artless smile, changing her features back to those of a dangerously beautiful woman. 'I have luxurious tastes – even more than you – and while I can and when I can I intend to indulge them.'

Latour grinned. 'Something like your taste in men, *ma petite?* By the way, where is that hulk of yours who drives you around?'

She smiled secretively. 'He has had certain – ah – qualities that have interested me. But I am making him just specifically my driver from now on. Where is he? Drinking some-where until I need him again, I suppose.'

Latour shook his head. 'And no doubt resenting every moment you are spending here with me. Watch him, my lovely. The pain of rejection sometimes turns into violence.'

She tossed her head. 'There is no man I can't handle.'

He threw back his head and laughed. 'Ah, you are *a femme fatale*, *cherie*, a coquette, an enchantress. *Le bon Dieu* have mercy on the man you really decide to bend completely to your will.'

She brushed his words aside. 'Eugene, we have to get together again and work out our plans completely. De la Huerta won't wait forever for his beef on the hoof.'

'Agreed, *ma belle*. We will get them to him and wish him and his troops *bon appetit*.'

Out at the Slash C, Sullivan gazed about at the furnishings of the lounge room. Every-thing was big and comfortable but the outstanding feature was the grand piano at one side of the room.

Theodora Cavendish followed his gaze. 'Curly had it brought from 'Frisco for me.' She walked across to the instrument. Sulli-van watched her with appreciation. She was wearing a silken gown with a train flowing across the floor behind her. The tightness of the cut emphasized every curve of her body.

Her hair was piled high on her head, a lustrous ebony heap set off by ear-rings and a necklace both made of pearls. He was not used to having his breath taken away but it was happening right now.

She sat down at the piano and ran her hands over the keys in expert fashion. She lifted her head and began to sing.

'My love is like a red red rose
That's newly sprung in June:
My love is like the melodie
That's sweetly played in tune.
So fair art thou, my bonnie lass,
So deep in love am I;
And I will love thee still, my dear,
Till a' the seas gang dry...'

As she finished she closed with a soft chord on the keys. She turned to Sullivan. 'How did that appeal to your aesthetic sense, Marshal?'

Sullivan was silent a moment. She stared, waiting and smiling. He said slowly, 'Nearly as much as the beauty of the singer.'

She raised her eyebrows. 'Ah – not only a strong man but also a gallant.' She got up from the piano and moved back to sit down opposite him. 'Tell me about yourself, Marshal. Did you ever marry?'

He shook his head. 'No. I never found anyone who inspired me like the girl did the man who wrote that song.'

She half-closed her eyes. 'Ah, yes, Robbie Burns. Well, Robbie was one who, as we say, played the field. Maybe you've done that, Marsh–'

He corrected her. 'Martin.'

She smiled. 'Martin. Maybe it's been a case of saloon girls a-plenty but never a bride. So you never met anyone who really broke down your defences?'

Sullivan's voice was strong yet quiet. 'Not until tonight.'

She sat back in her chair, the fingers of one hand raised to rest gently against her cheek. 'Oh.' Her smile widened a little. 'Maybe I'd better sing another song, not a love song this time. Something about the open air, galloping horses, battle.'

'Don't do that. You've created an atmosphere and I like it.'

She stared back at him silently. 'You know, I've never met a man quite like you. Curly loved me, I'm sure, and I could get him to do anything I wanted. And there have been other men, too. But you...'

She got slowly to her feet. She said deliberately, 'I'm going into another room and you're at liberty to follow me.' She went across the room and through a door, her body moving with an easy, sensuous grace. After a little while Sullivan got to his feet. As he followed her he was already unbuttoning his shirt.

Jim Moran sat opposite Sullivan in the office of the jailhouse. He said briefly, 'No more rustlin' from Ned Munro's Flyin' M. Maybe it was jist some small-time thief gittin' hisself a dollar or two.'

Sullivan said, 'We'll keep an eye on 'em but could be it's like you said. Anything else?'

Moran picked his teeth a moment. 'Yeah. Yeah. I got a feelin' about Eugene Latour. Never done anythin' much wrong since he came to this town a year or two ago an' bought that saloon. But he's been a gambler an' I jist figger that maybe he ain't past puttin' over a fast deal. Jist got a feelin'.'

'Well, we'll keep an eye on him, too. Anything else?' Moran shifted uneasily. He gave Sullivan a quick look and then glanced away. Sullivan said easily, 'Spit it out, Jim.'

Moran cleared his throat. 'Ain't fer me to go tellin' you how to handle your personal affairs, Marshal, but I been thinkin' that maybe if you was to ease down before you git – uh – maybe a mite too close to the boss of the Slash C. She was bad medicine for Curly an' I figger he wasn't the first she sorta used up.'

There was silence for a moment. Sullivan broke it. 'You're right, Jim. It is not your business to tell me how to go about my private life. I'll thank you not to contemplate doing that again.'

Moran got to his feet and nodded stiffly. 'OK, Marshal, OK.' He turned to go.

Sullivan raised his voice. 'I want to say something else. I admire the way you are staying away from the liquor. You're getting to be a first-class deputy. And although I didn't like your advice, I appreciate your concern.'

Moran gave him a quick salute and walked away. Sullivan sat there for a while, thinking. Maybe her shiny black hair might turn into a silken noose for unwary men, but he would risk it.

SIX

The light of the camp fire threw the monstrous shadow of the huge man across the rock behind him. He took a great gulp of steaming coffee from the mug in his hand.

The other man squatting at the fire opposite him growled uneasily, 'Maybe we ought not to be buildin' fires, Rube, with them rustled beeves on our hands.'

The big man jeered, 'Jess, you always had a little case of the heebie-jeebies when we been doin' somethin' like this. Jest fergit about it. If I do say so, we did a real neat job of thievin' them cows. That rancher ain't gunna know they are gone fer days. It's a big spread an' line riders can only cover so much ground per day.'

He grumbled, 'Never thought we'd have to go so fur to git them but then in Californy we ain't livin' in a real cattle-rich state. Minin' changed all that.' He gave a thick-throated chuckle. 'But only gotta sneak over the border into Nevady or Arizony Territory now an' then an' we kin build up our tally.'

Jess Palmer enquired, 'What you figger them Mex rebs payin' Latour an' the Cavendish woman fer these cows?'

Big Rube said shrewdly, 'More money than we gunna see. Prob'ly what the trail drivers git at the railhead – twenty dollars per head.'

His brother leered, 'Figger we got a chance to sell 'em to the greasers an' take the money ourselves?'

Big Rube spat into the fire. 'Don't think I ain't considered it. But when the big sale comes off I understand Latour is gunna be on hand – an' maybe the woman, too. But I hear tell the Frog has hired a gunnie to watch out for his interests. An' I hear also that the gunnie is Gil Kelso.'

Jess Palmer jerked his head up. 'Kelso? Hey, he got more notches on his gun than a woodpecker coulda put there.'

Big Rube nodded. 'Yeah. Ain't no real good sense in tanglin' with him.' He stared into the fire thoughtfully. 'But maybe there might be a chance to make a little more profit fer ourselves even with that killer around.' He brightened. 'But what we are gittin' ain't chicken feed. They are payin' us more dollars than we seen in a long time.' He chuckled. 'An' all fer doin' jest what comes nachally to us.'

He said abruptly, 'Time we bed down fer a hour or two. We gotta relieve Caleb an' Sammy watchin' them beeves.' He yawned. 'Gotta git them to Horton's spread as quick as we can. The sooner we can build up a big tally the quicker the sale will come off an' we will git the rest of our dough.'

They both lurched up from the dying fire and spread out their blankets near the rocks. Soon two sounds that might have come from the snouts of sleeping boar hogs filled the air.

Jerry Owens cleared his throat and spoke up. 'Marshal, you know a young lady name of Faith Archer?'

Sullivan turned from the desk to look at him. He said curiously, 'That I do. The daughter of Judge Archer. A right handsome young woman if ever there was one and with an equally pleasing manner.' He shook his head. 'Like the judge said, how he happened to sire her remains a miracle that only the good Lord can work.'

The boy cleared his throat again. 'Well, I met her on the street. She dropped some packages and I helped her pick them up. We got talking and I told her I was one of your deputies. Well, sir, she asked me to have a meal with her and her folks.'

Sullivan surveyed him carefully. 'You continue to surprise me.' He asked abruptly, 'How old are you, kid?'

'Eighteen years and two months, Marshal.'

Sullivan nodded. 'And she is seventeen, the judge told me.' He ran his eyes over the boy. 'You know, Jerome Owens, I don't want you to have to buy a bigger size hat to fit your head but you are a good-looking young feller. Fresh face, good mop of curly hair, look just like a non-smoking, non-drinking, clean-cut young man ought to look.'

His smile came through suddenly, again clearing the ice from his eyes. 'A froggie would a-wooing go...' Hop to it, kid. That girl is really something.'

Eugene Latour poured the whiskey into the glass. The other man called, 'Whoa, there. That's enough. Two fingers. And just the one drink.'

The Frenchman smiled. 'I thought, *mon ami*, that you would be a man of some capacity when it came to hard liquor.'

The other man's voice was flat and toneless. 'Takes the edge off both the speed and direction. I've seen too many gunnies killed because they held a glass in their hand more often than a pistol.'

The speaker was about medium height, sparely built, not much more than jockey size. He wore a fairly heavy black moustache, almost hiding his mouth. His whole appearance including clothes and physique was neat and clean but in no way extraordinary.

But when one looked at his eyes it was different. They were sharp, penetrating, as if they could see through solid things, around doorways, behind him and to the side all at once. Apart from that they were totally without expression. It was hard to tell what colour they were. One might have guessed at a slatey grey.

He moved one hand to pick up the drink. His touch was light, graceful, dexterous. It might have been the hand of a conjurer.

Latour sipped at his own drink. He said reflectively, 'Of course, I may have no need for you at all.'

The other man said in the same toneless voice, 'But you will pay me the rest of what you owe me even if I never have to put my hand near my pistol butt.'

The Frenchman smiled again. 'You will

get your money, have no fear. I am engaged on an enterprise that apart from my saloon profits will ensure you of that.' He smiled more widely. 'But, of course, Gil Kelso and his – ah – artistry do not come cheap.'

The gunman clipped out, 'But they get results.' He mused, 'You got a marshal name of Sullivan. That is, Second-shot Sullivan?'

'*Oui*. You know of him?'

Kelso inclined his head. 'Heard of him, yeah. Don't believe most of it.' His eyes narrowed down to the slits of a marksman eyeing his target. 'Maybe I'll meet up with him.'

Latour said thoughtfully, 'I would not advise it unless totally necessary. He has a way with a gun.'

Kelso said softly, 'We'll see.'

Latour lifted his glass. 'To our arrangement.'

Kelso drank silently. Latour thought, his mind eternally seems to be on deadlier things. He shivered a little but at the same time congratulated himself. He had an arm of destruction at his side that ought to keep things pretty secure for things like the venture on which he and Theodora Cavendish were engaged.

Miriam Archer, still handsome in her middle age but prim and circumspect in all her ways, enquired distantly, 'And what are your prospects as a deputy – ah – *Mister* Owens?'

Jerry Owens smiled his youthful, engaging smile that appeared not to be especially engaging to Mrs Archer. 'Well, ma'am, I figure that if I watch and learn from Marshal Sullivan I am going to one day maybe get to be a marshal myself.'

The judge's wife twisted her mouth a little distastefully. 'A violent man. Those dead men he brought in–' She shuddered briefly. 'And a violent profession. Surely there are better ways of making a living.'

Jerry said stoutly, 'The way I see it, ma'am, it's an honourable trade. Keeping the law, making disturbers of the peace behave, protecting the decent citizens, upholding the United States government.'

Miriam Archer sniffed a little. The judge spoke up. 'The boy's right, my dear. It is a highly needful occupation.' He frowned a little. 'Only trouble is, a good number of its practitioners live on borrowed time. It is a dangerous profession.'

Mrs Archer looked triumphantly across the table at a girl with a long train of golden hair, sparkling blue eyes and a face as fresh and appealing as only healthy youth could make it. The girl responded immediately. 'But, Mother, there's danger in other things, too. Why, Father here–' she glanced at the judge – 'has had death threats from offenders he has sentenced.' She smiled warmly. 'And he's still with us, bless him.'

The judge's face relaxed into a look of deep affection. 'That's so, my dear. And I intend to be with you a while yet. Long enough,' he looked at her benignly, 'to see you married to a good man and settled down.'

The girl smiled but there was a strong note of independence in her voice. 'To someone, no doubt, hand-picked for me by yourself and Mamma. But, you know, Father, there's a new spirit in society. Women are beginning to decide things for themselves. For instance, they are starting to demand why they are not permitted to enter professions formerly dominated by men.' She grinned mischievously. 'Why, one day we may even see female peace officers – gun in hand and all.'

Her mother protested, 'Faith, don't talk such – such vulgar nonsense.'

Faith shook her head. She said gently, 'Mamma, you love me I know but sometimes it can get a little too confining. By the way, I'm not going back to that ladies' college you sent me to.'

Both her parents sat upright. The judge rapped, 'Why, Daughter, you can't do this–'

Mrs Archer murmured weakly, 'Faith, Faith, what are you saying...?'

The girl said cheerily, 'Simply that that place was just a sort of factory turning out women as the faculty thought they ought to be – unthinking little dolls whose only ambition is to be replicas of their rather snobbish, unimaginative elders. I am going to find myself a job – in a law office preferably. That's something I'd like to study.'

Miriam Archer threw up her hands. 'Law? That's only for men.'

Faith shook her head. 'Right now, Mamma, yes. But the day is coming...' She reached across and patted her mother's hand. 'But we are leaving our guest right out of this. Let's get Esmeralda to remove the dishes while we go into the other room.'

A thin, gaunt woman, evidently long employed about the household and very privileged, came in from the kitchen, grumbling. 'Land sakes, thought you was gunna sit around here talkin' back an' forth all night. Let me git them plates cleaned up.'

It was later when Jerry Owens was leaving

81

that Faith Archer walked with him to the front gate and said encouragingly, 'Don't worry about my folks. They are a little what one might call conservative.' She gave him a steady look. 'They can't see in you the sort of material they're looking for in a husband for me.' She blushed a little. 'That's – that's maybe a little embarrassing for you, as a permanent relationship might be the furthest thing from your mind, but I like you, Jerry Owens, and you can call on me any time you like.'

Jerry stared back at her and gulped. 'Miss Archer – uh, Faith – I think you are the prettiest girl I ever did see and I sure do want to see you again.' She took his hand and squeezed it and turned to go. As she did she grinned again.

'Don't take all that free and unfettered woman stuff I was spouting back there without a grain of salt. I was just laying it on for them so they would clearly get the idea I am not going to be told whom I ought or ought not to entertain as a male friend.' She added strongly, 'You're in a good honourable job, Jerry, and don't let anyone tell you differently.'

The boy walked back to his lodging house, looking up at the stars and wondering why they had never looked so big and bright and fancy before.

Back at the house the older two were talking, Miriam Archer agitatedly. 'This Owens boy, Achilles – young, penniless, no real prospects except maybe a bullet from a bad man–'

The judge was solemn. 'Hush, my dear. Nothing's come of it yet. Faith, despite all her liberated woman talk, has got a good head on her shoulders. She will do the sensible thing.' But as he said it he was wishing right then that they had raised a boy. A girl could be such a problem. Girls talked so much and, unfortunately, sometimes they said things you couldn't find answers for. He brushed it from his mind. Faith was a clear thinker and she would finally see sense.

Big Rube and his brothers kept on hazing the cows through the fence that had been let down for them to pass beyond.

A couple of riders were waiting on the other side, one of them a thin, bony man who sat his horse in a manner that showed he was not a born cowman. Big Rube drew abreast of him. 'Horton?' The other nodded. Rube Palmer grunted. 'Here's the first consignment.' He chuckled. 'Rustled from

83

some of the best cow outfits in Californy an' adjoinin' borders. An' there's more comin'.'

The other man, with a face like a skull stripped of flesh and eyes that darted back and forth, seeing everything and missing nothing in the manner of a man born for the gaming table, said in a sharp voice, 'There had better be more. There's a mighty big passel of hungry greasers the other side of the border.' He asked, 'Any trouble on the way down?'

The big man leered. 'Nary a sign. The only trouble might be with them greasers. They are mighty good at wrigglin' out of a deal by doin' somethin' shifty.'

Horton rapped, 'They better not try it.' He shot a warning look at Rube Palmer. 'And neither had anyone else. I had word from Latour that he has hired Gil Kelso to look after his and Theodora Cavendish's interests. The last I heard of Kelso he had run out of room on his pistol to carve another notch.'

Big Rube tried to look as honest as he could. 'Sure, sure. We are happy with our cut. All we want to see is the cows delivered as per contract and the rest of our money paid to us.'

Horton clipped out, 'That's good to hear.

No sense in trying to deal from the bottom of the pack when you've already got a winning hand.'

Big Rube took a closer glance at this man in the dark. He looked nearly as dangerous as Gil Kelso. Big Rube sighed. Seemed like he and his brothers could only count on what they had agreed to be paid. Oh, well, another time and an easier mark. There was some hard riding ahead but the pay was still pretty good.

SEVEN

Jim Moran said, 'Ain't only Ned Munro. More cows been rustled. Hear tell, too, that one/two ranches been raided 'cross the border. Almost seems like someone is gittin' together a big herd to sell some place. Lotta brand changin' must be goin' on.'

'Rustlers,' said Sullivan, 'have been with us since the good Lord put horns on four-legged beasts. We don't want to get panicked into thinking there is a big-scale scheme operating under master minds. Still, thieving is thieving and it needs to be stopped. You any ideas about who might be involved?'

Moran sucked in his lower lip. He drawled, 'Well, seems like the Palmer boys 'pear to be away from their broken-down spread a lot. Still, that ain't unusual. They git up to all kinds of fancy capers. Not only here but over the border to Nevada. Seems they robbed a bank there once but never got proved.' He said drily, 'Maybe someone took a look at that rogue elephant, Big Rube, an' decided better not to witness agin him.' He grinned at the marshal. 'But you shaved his tusks a little. Maybe they need shavin' a mite more.'

Sullivan grunted, 'Maybe. But until we find out for sure who might be doing this thieving we can't do much about it. But keep nosing around. Bound to pick up a clue somewhere.'

Moran nodded. He turned to go but stopped at the door. He coughed and cleared his throat. 'Miz Cavendish – she well?'

Sullivan gave him a cold stare, his eyes suddenly icier than ever. 'Very. But why ask me?'

Jim Moran cleared his throat again. 'Well, Marshal, jest on account of you seein' so much of her.'

'Anything wrong with that?'

The deputy drawled, 'Only if it turns out

that maybe Eugene Latour don't like it. Or maybe Ben Carson. Miz Cavendish got a way of gittin' her men to sorta dislike each other. Sometimes they git real mean about it.'

Sullivan said, voice as icy as his eyes, 'I don't need advice as if I was a kid fresh out of school, Deputy. Whatever comes along in my life I can handle. I would appreciate it if you did not bring up this subject again.'

Moran lifted a hand in acknowledgment. 'OK, Marshal, but I still say you are mixin' with a most unusual an' un-pree-dictable lady.' He walked out the door.

The ice in Sullivan's eyes took a while to thaw. He turned to his desk and thumbed through some papers roughly with a touch of anger. But he knew that at the back of his mind there was the same nagging thought that Moran had put into words.

Even when her train of long black hair was loosed and tumbling about his own bare shoulders, her arms open and willing, he had a feeling that this woman would never be one man's property. There was something about her that told of a perverseness, an untamed quality, that somehow kept her aloof even in the most passionate embrace.

He cleared his mind of the thought and

concentrated on his desk work but he knew the thought would return. Theodora Cavendish was a woman who demanded and took but never gave fully of herself in return.

That night Sullivan made the patrol of the town alone. He smiled as he thought how he had given the boy, Jerry, the night off to go visit the Archers at Faith's invitation.

He stopped smiling for a moment as he considered how young Jerry was not really welcomed by Faith's parents. Sullivan himself could see the strong potential the youth had for becoming a lawman of the top order but the judge and his wife evidently were looking for a man of what they called substance for their daughter.

Sullivan smiled again a little crookedly. A man of substance to them meant someone with a college education, who wore the right clothes, said the right things and knew how to conduct himself at a soirée where the guests were known as ladies and gentlemen.

Jerry Owens didn't have those attributes but he was ambitious as far as his job went and honestly smitten by Faith Archer. And, thought Sullivan, that pretty peach of a girl was surely smitten by him.

Later on his patrol Sullivan walked into the Bonne Chance. Not that there was any outburst of unacceptable behaviour there more than anywhere else but it was his job to check.

He noted that Lilian Blainey was finishing her act and was leaving the stage set up at one end of the saloon. He strolled down there. He had an unusual urge to maybe talk to her again. He had realized that he liked her outspoken candour and her confidence that she had nothing to be ashamed of in her way of making a living.

She was wearing an outfit that displayed, he noticed, her very well-shaped legs. As he reached the end of the stage he saw that Latour was standing there.

As the girl came past the closing curtain the Frenchman, smiling, reached out a hand and caressed her thigh. Lilian Blainey thrust his hand away violently, her eyes blazing. She burst out, 'Don't ever do that again.' She stormed off to her dressing-room. Latour, an ugly look on his face and oblivious to Sullivan, went after her menacingly.

Sullivan followed automatically. The girl had gone into the dressing-room and the marshal saw the Frenchman enter it hurriedly and then slam the door behind him. There came the sound of a face being slapped and the girl's sudden cry of shock.

The Frenchman's voice rose in a stream of abuse.

Sullivan opened the door and went in. Lilian Blainey stood before her dressing-table mirror, hand raised to a reddening cheek, both shock and anger in her gaze. Latour swung around to face the marshal, his face twisted with a rage that totally destroyed his handsomeness. Sullivan said coolly, 'Not the way to treat a lady, *m'sieur.*'

The Frenchman glared. 'Mind your own business, Marshal.'

Sullivan insisted, 'This *is* my business. I don't like to see anyone pushed around. Seems to me that's what you are doing right now to this girl.'

Latour hissed, 'She is in my employ. I treat my staff as I please.'

'Not if it means forcing your attentions on them. And that's what I have just seen you doing.'

Latour struggled for self-control. Regaining some semblance of it, he walked to the door. He flung back at Sullivan, 'Keeping disturbers of the peace in order is your proper vocation, Marshal.'

Sullivan said mildly, 'Seems to me you were disturbing this young lady's peace. I'd advise you not to try it again.' Latour slammed the door shut once again as he went out, the silence of his rage more voluble than a noisy outburst.

Sullivan shifted his gaze to the girl. 'Don't know why I keep doing this for you. I guess a man's approaches are all in a day's work in your line of business.'

The girl's face lost the glance of appreciation that had been dawning there. She said frigidly, 'Can't get your mind out of that one-track groove, can you, Marshal – that saloon girls are all vicious harpies wrecking and plundering men? Some one of us must have crossed you up badly.'

'No. All I ever got from them was what I paid for. I made sure of that. And at the same time I kept my pockets buttoned up.' He asked curtly, 'Latour try that often?'

She shook her head. 'Only tonight. But once is enough.' She turned to the dressing-table and took a derringer pistol out of a drawer. It was a four-barrelled Sharps, chased and ornamented with a tracery of flowers and foliage.

She said mockingly, 'Here's another black mark against me in your eyes, Marshal. My father was a gambler and when he died he bequeathed this to me. Let me tell you, if *M'sieur* gets too insistent I may have to use it on him. When I'm in ordinary dress I carry it on me all the time.'

Sullivan cautioned, 'Those things are little but lethal. I don't want to have to arrest you for murder – even though the corpse might only be that of a French lecher.' He said abruptly, 'Can I buy you a drink?'

She gave him a cool glance. 'It may surprise you, Marshal, but I don't drink. And now, if you'll excuse me, I have to prepare for another performance.'

As Sullivan walked away outside he was thinking, this girl is full of surprises. And somehow he was very curious to discover how many more surprises he might find in her.

Judge Achilles Archer looked across the desk in his study at Jerry Owens. He took a cigar from a box on his desk and offered Jerry one. The boy shook his head. 'Don't smoke, sir.'

The judge sighed, 'Wise man. I've sent many good dollars up in cigar smoke.' He lit up and puffed away. 'Now, Jerry, I have excused ourselves to the ladies and asked you in here because I want to have a very serious chat with you.'

The boy gazed back at him, open-faced

and cheery. 'Yes, sir.'

As the judge gazed at him in return he felt a sudden twinge of regret at what he was going to say. This boy had such an honest, decent look about him. But he dismissed the thought and went on. 'Son, I don't want to be hard on you but I want to discourage you from seeing my daughter. You see, my wife and I have very positive ideas about whom we would like Faith to marry. We have in mind some young man with – ah – prospects. We are thinking in terms of a doctor, a lawyer, maybe a young fellow already solidly established in some business career.'

He sighed for a moment with an inescapable feeling that he was perhaps sounding like a socially conscious snob. The boy's reply shook him a little.

'Doesn't it matter what Faith might want?'

The judge harrumphed, 'Well, yes, of course, but Faith is young, inexperienced, naive. Her mother and I feel that we have a more accurate sense of what is the right thing.' He took a sidelong glance at the boy. 'You understand what I'm saying, Jerry?'

The boy's face had turned rigid. He said stiffly, 'Yes, Judge, you've made it quite plain.'

'Well, now,' the judge changed the subject,

'let's talk about something else – like, for instance, this rustling that's been going on. The marshal any closer to finding the culprits?'

Jerry shook his head. He said dully, 'No, sir, he isn't.'

The judge wagged his head. 'That's a pity. Let me tell you something. If he–' he waved his hand indulgently – 'or either of his deputies for that matter, should bring those thieves to book the town and myself would be extremely grateful. We would know that we have lawmen with us who are really doing their job. Let me say that it would raise our opinion of them greatly.'

He added, 'Not that we don't appreciate you even now but if these rascals were apprehended, well, we would all regard that as a very fine service.' He got to his feet. 'But I think we should be rejoining the ladies.'

Jerry stood up. He said clearly, 'I think I'll go right now, Judge.'

The older man was taken aback. 'But, Jerry, surely not. You mustn't take what I said as a personal criticism. It's just that–'

The boy said clearly, 'I am more concerned with what Faith thinks, Judge. But I've got things to do.'

The judge stared. 'Well, if that's how you feel.' He turned to another door. 'You can go out this way if you like.'

Outside Jerry Owens quickened his step. He hurried back to his lodgings, went to his room and changed his clothes to his ordinary garb – woollen shirt, worn levis and worn riding boots. He picked up a mackinaw and pulled it on. He would need it.

He went back to the empty jailhouse and strode to the weapon rack. He took out a Winchester rifle and then on second thoughts went to the marshal's desk. He pulled open a drawer and slipped his hand around a spare Smith & Wesson .44 revolver he knew was there and shoved it down the top of his levis.

He filled up on ammunition for both weapons from boxes in the drawers in the desk and hurried out the door.

When he headed out of town a short time later on the horse the marshal had supplied him with there was a determined set to his jaw. He was a lawman set to bring in law-breakers.

A couple of campfires behind him, Jerry Owens rode on into the early morning. The sun was beginning to come up and it was not yet clear daylight but Jerry was eager to move on. His thoughts were on other things than the heat that was coming and his hopes were high.

He had found tracks, been given some information on the way from a Mexican goatherd and he was hot on the trail. He was riding to catch up with them and see exactly where they were headed.

He knew he had passed the line over into Nevada where there was prime cattle and he was looking eagerly ahead.

Big Rube eased himself in the saddle. He said huskily, 'I gotta feelin' we got company.' He looked at Jess riding alongside him. 'You got that feelin', too?'

His thinner, slouch-shouldered brother nodded assent. 'Yeah, yeah. I got it, too.'

Big Rube looked at him scathingly. 'You always got it. You see sheriffs an' lawmen of ever' which kind behind ever' bunch of sage brush.' He jerked out, 'You an' Sammy go on. Me an' Caleb gunna take a look back along the trail.'

He swung his horse around and his brother Caleb, cursing a little at the break in their journey, turned back with him. They rode for a while silently, Caleb with a bad grace. Suddenly Big Rube's hoarse voice said, 'Whoa, there, Cal. We got company sure enough.'

Caleb Palmer looked up to see the rider coming towards them. Every now and then the rider looked down at the ground, following the trail of hoofmarks.

Big Rube said softly, 'We got a pursuer, a bloodhound on our trail. What we gotta do is discourage him.' He pulled his horse to a halt and dismounted. He led the animal to a patch of tall sage brush, six feet high with its grey leaves and buds of what would be small yellow flowers.

He signed to his brother to follow him. Caleb was not grumbling now and his beady eyes were alert. They left the horses behind them, reins hanging on the ground. Big Rube had taken a rifle out of his saddle boot. Crouching a little lower, he was still not visible to the oncoming rider.

He husked to his brother, 'That jigger ain't lookin' our way. He's too busy followin' our tracks. I'm gunna draw his attention.' He stood up, put rifle to shoulder and fired.

Jerry Owens came up in the saddle as if a giant had grabbed and yanked him. He tumbled to the ground, as silent as a shot bird. His horse, startled, reared and galloped away.

Big Rube strode forward. He reached the still figure and turned it over. There was a bullet hole in the chest, oozing blood. The boy's eyes were shut tight, his face drained and white as the victim of a vampire.

Big Rube boomed, 'Well, if it ain't that kid depitty.' He leaned down and pressed his shaggy head against the boy's chest. He stood up. 'Deader than Custer at the Little Big Horn. Let's git goin'.'

Caleb jerked out, 'What about his horse?' Big Rube shrugged his bear shoulders. 'Let it run. Maybe it will git home, maybe it won't. Sure thing this kid won't be headin' home an' that was our only problem. We'll drag him into the bushes an' leave him there. The buzzards will do the rest.'

Later, remounting, they rode on. The important thing was to get to that spread where they knew there were fat cattle waiting feeding on the all-year-round grazing.

EIGHT

Sullivan pushed on along the trail. He muttered as he rode, 'Those cattle thieves are sure covering a lot of territory to rustle cows. They must be aiming to sell an awful lot of stolen beeves to someone somewhere. Must have a pretty good knowledge of trails, water holes and grazing spots in shifting them from one faraway place to another.'

He stopped talking to himself and kept riding on, knowing that he had crossed the border a while since. A huge clump of six foot high sagebrush hove into view. He could see a tiny creek nearby and some scant grazing.

And then he saw the horse, moving quietly around as it snatched at the grass, still saddled and bridled. He recognized it as the boy's mount.

'Now, where–' His half-asked question was soon answered. He saw the twisted body lying there, semi-conscious. He got down off his mount quickly. Jerry Owens was lying curled up like an embryo inside the womb.

His hands were clutching a canteen.

Sullivan figured quickly that the boy had somehow staggered to his horse and got to the canteen strapped to the saddle. The animal may have run off at first but had returned to the grass nearby.

The boy had dried blood on his hands from clutching at the gaping gunshot wound that Sullivan saw as he turned him gently over.

Jerry's eyes flickered open sightlessly at the movement, a groan of pain coming from him. After he had cleaned the ugly wound with water from the creek and roughly bandaged it, Sullivan muttered, 'Got to get you back, kid. Maybe the sawbones in Estrada can save you yet.'

Getting the boy on the back of his horse and tying him there was no easy task. The boy flopped uselessly, a stricken thing, life barely visible. Sullivan moved off, leading Jerry's horse by the reins. He couldn't move all that fast and he hoped he would be in time.

He looked across at the limp figure on the horse moving alongside him. He said aloud, 'So, you wanted to be a big lawman and help capture the cow thieves to impress Faith Archer's family. Well, kid, you bit off too big a mouthful for your young jaws. But we'll just have to finish what you started.'

Back in Estrada the doctor looked gravely at the boy. 'Damn near blasted a tunnel through him with that slug. No sign of it, so it passed right through him. It's good it hasn't lodged in him, causing more trouble. But it's done a lot of damage in passing through.'

He looked soberly at Sullivan. 'Tell you this, Marshal – maybe you are going to have to look around for another deputy.'

Sullivan said quietly, 'I hope not, Doc. I have sort of come to value this one, fool kid and all as he is, just do your best.'

He left the surgery with dark thoughts in his mind. Before it had just been a few cattle stolen from one rancher. Now it was assuming the aspect of a mighty far-spread raid, crossing frontiers and boundaries.

And the big thing was that a lawman, however minor, had been shot down while in the act of doing his duty. Sullivan's eyes took on a look that would have made an ice-floe appear temperate. *This* he would rectify.

Jim Moran hesitated a moment. The barman in the Bonne Chance said again, 'Have one on the house, Jim. The boss believes in being on the right side of the law. He likes to offer peace officers little courtesies.'

Moran had been dry a while. He licked his lips. He said involuntarily, 'OK, then. I guess the liquor here is a little better than the rotgut in some of the saloons in town.' He downed the drink and sighed satisfiedly.

The barman urged, 'Have another. The first two are always free to local lawmen.'

Moran, about to move off, slowly turned back. 'That so? Must be a new custom. Well, if it's free that's about as cheap as you can git it.' He tossed down another drink.

He looked at the empty glass and then suddenly made up his mind. He said curtly, 'Give me a bottle.' The barman grinned and took down a bottle from a shelf. Jim Moran picked it up, retaining the glass, and moved to a nearby table. He settled down with the bottle.

Latour, watching from a distance, smiled. It was good to know the Achilles' heel of any likely opponent. An hour later Jim Moran was still drinking in the Bonne Chance.

Latour as he passed by gave the deputy a thoughtful look. Maybe it was time he encouraged the man to move off. He had thoughts of other occasions when alcohol had stirred Moran into ugly action.

Through a nearby door a smallish, neat figure appeared. It was Gil Kelso, gazing about him as he moved, a wary, catlike tread in his walk, expressionless eyes taking in everything about him with the minute observation of an Indian reading track sign.

Jim Moran lifted his head and gazed across at the newcomer. The deputy's eyes had taken on a dull look, the lacklustre appearance of the heavy drinker. His mouth had tightened and there was an increasing hostility in his stare.

He raised his voice. 'Hey, you, Kelso, what you doin' in our town? Why don't you take your artillery elsewhere? Only notches you're gunna find right here might be on someone else's gun when they ventilate you.'

The gunman turned slowly to face the deputy. His voice was as expressionless as his eyes. 'You have a loud mouth, friend.'

Moran got slowly to his feet, slightly unsteady. 'Yeah, an' I got a tin star to back it up. Why don't you git on whatever bronc you rustled recently an' head outa town? We don't want weasels like you around.'

Kelso had tensed himself into a near crouch. His voice was quiet but penetrating. 'Like I said, you have a big mouth. If you close it right now I'll overlook what you've been saying.'

Moran jeered, 'Backin' down a little, huh? Why, you sneakin' little backshooter, I ain't scared of you–' He shot a clumsy hand down towards the butt of his gun.

Kelso's weapon was in his hand with the speed of a gambler flicking a card across a table. His first shot grazed Moran's gun-hand, scoring a crimson slash across it and numbing the deputy's fingers.

His following shots were aimed at Moran's feet and made the deputy prance in comical fashion as he tried to avoid the bullets. One shot had torn away the toe of one of his boots. With a wounded gun-hand the deputy had no chance of firing in return.

There were only a few customers in the saloon as it was morning but a faint ripple of laughter ran through them. The deputy looked ludicrous as he stood there, hopelessly beaten to the draw by an opponent who scorned him to the extent that he would not make a duel of it.

Kelso's voice was a taunting whiplash of derision. 'You still got your star, lawman. I could have shot that off you, too. Go home and polish it. Maybe it'll bring you better luck next time.'

Jim Moran glared, eyes seething with

shamed resentment. He turned and walked unsteadily to the batwing doors, clumsily wrapping a rag from his pocket around his grazed hand as he went. The laughter grew louder as he left.

Kelso snapped, 'You all saw him draw on me. Coulda killed him but I am a peaceable man.' The laughter died down. No one wanted to pursue the subject.

The gunman went over to the bar and as the barman saw him coming he got him a drink. Kelso threw it down and went out the door he had come in by. Latour, watching, thought maybe he has taught the law to be a little wary. But at the same time he considered the fact that Sullivan was a different proposition to his alcohol-prone deputy.

Still, he assured himself, Kelso had a gunhand that had just shown itself to be born of the union of lightning and quicksilver. He smiled confidently as he went about his business.

Faith Archer looked down at the silent, white face of the boy, his eyes closed, his breath hardly audible. She was anxiety to her fingertips. 'Doctor, is he – will he–'

Doctor John Freeman shook his head. 'Might as well have been shot by a cannon.

Hole in him big enough to drive a steer through. But I'll say this – if clean living and a good, strong, farmer's-boy body will do enough he may yet pull through.' He looked at her over his spectacles. 'Faith, I calculate you have a special interest in this lad?'

The girl kept looking down at the prone, deadly-still figure. 'I – I find him honest, decent with good ambition and fine motives. I like him very much.'

'H'm. Your folks feel that way?'

She gave him a worried glance. 'No. Not exactly. But I'm sure they are going to appreciate what he did – going after those rustlers lone-handed like that.'

The doctor sighed. 'The damn foolhardy cavalier confidence of youth.' He wagged his head. 'But you got to admire the boy. He's sure got some grit.' He added gently, 'Maybe you'd better go, girl. Not much you can really do.'

She pulled up a chair and sat down. She said firmly, 'I can wait and watch, Doctor. That's if you don't mind.' Not waiting for his answer her eyes were fixed steadily on the boy.

The doctor shot her a keen look and gave in. 'All right, lass. You can stay a while.' His face grew a little grimmer. 'But it might only be to hold his hand while he passes on to where they don't have any stolen cattle or rustlers who wantonly shoot down decent boys.'

She didn't hear him, her eyes fastened with steady fixedness on the still figure. The doctor moved out quietly. Here was a watcher whose deep concern that the boy should live could be nothing but an aid to what seemed almost impossible recovery.

Jim Moran sat alone that night in his room at the lodging-house. He had another bottle and he poured himself a drink every now and then. He downed each mouthful with a sullen savagery that typified his ugly mood.

Sullivan had been to see him and had been short and brutal in his approach. He had told the deputy that he was on his last chance, either sober up for good or hand in his star. The marshal had assured him in a sharp, clipped manner that he knew all about Gil Kelso and his reputation but the way the deputy had approached the gun-man was not in the best interests of law and order.

To sour things even more for Jim Moran, he knew that what the marshal had said was right and that all he had done was again make himself a laughing stock. But instead of putting it out of his mind he was allowing it to rankle.

The liquor was now working heavily on him and suddenly he came to a wild decision. He would play his own hand his own way. He pushed the bottle aside and put his hand down to the gun holstered at his right hip. He lifted the hand and pulled the bandage from it with a wince.

The wound had really only been a graze and painful at the time but now the pain had receded and all that was there now was a faint throb.

If the deputy had been in his right senses he would have paused to consider the deadeye accuracy that had allowed Kelso to aim at just the top of the hand merely to temporarily deprive the owner of its use. But the alcohol he had consumed had slowed up his reasoning process. He pushed the bottle aside and got to his feet.

In a minute or two he was headed for the Bonne Chance saloon. Reaching there, he stood out in the middle of the street, swaying just a little. He lifted his head and bawled out, 'Hey, you in there, Kelso, you yeller-livered coyote, I'm callin' you out. Come on out an' be ready to draw.'

There was a sudden quiet inside the saloon. Jim Moran bawled again, 'Scared, Kelso? You ain't put my pistol hand out of action. I'm ready to beat you to the draw any time. You hear me? I'm callin' you out, you skunk.'

There was almost complete silence inside the saloon despite the blaze of lights. Then suddenly there were light footsteps and a form appeared through the batwing doors, slim, neat, small, walking on the feet of a cautious, wary cougar. Jim Moran blinked at the sudden glare of light through the doors.

He bellowed, 'Draw, you son-of-a-' His hand flew down to his gun.

There were two shots. Moran, his hand still merely resting on his gun butt, began to sway. It was not the stagger of a drunk but of a dead man. If it had not been night and one had stood close to him the two holes, one in his chest, the other in his stomach, could have been seen, the flesh drilled with scrupulous accuracy.

The deputy fell, like an actor rehearsing a death scene and sprawled on the ground, his last act as a lawman over and done.

Gil Kelso, still standing in the doorway, reholstered his gun. He called aloud, 'You all saw it. He insulted me, he called me out, he drew on me and I shot him before he shot me. Ain't no lawman, no judge, can pin anything on me for this.' He turned and walked back inside, leaving whoever to pick up the body outside.

Faith Archer met Martin Sullivan's eyes across the still unconscious body of Jerry Owens. She said breathlessly, 'I heard about your deputy, Jim Moran. Nothing you can do?'

Sullivan drew in a slow breath. 'No. He signed his own death warrant doing what he did. Kelso, according to all the witnesses and, I suppose, according to law, merely acted in self-defence. The fact that he killed a drunken man whom he had already slightly disabled doesn't count. Nor the fact that it was a peace officer. They are not supposed to get themselves into such very unlawful and suicidal situations.'

He looked down at the boy concernedly. 'How's he coming?'

Faith, a suspicious dampness in her eyes, said low voiced, 'The doctor says it's amazing how he is hanging on. He says he thinks perhaps Jerry knows I'm at his side. He says he thinks it helps.'

Sullivan said firmly, 'I'm sure it does.

Greatly.' He looked again at the boy. 'He's lucky. Got a woman who cares for him.'

She gave him a quick glance. 'Haven't you? I've heard that Theodora Cavendish and you–'

He finished for her, drily, 'Find some – ah –satisfaction in each other. Actually, she is a very attractive woman. But sitting devotedly by a sick man's side, well–' he smiled quietly at her – 'that seems to be only for girls like you.'

He went to leave. 'Keep watch over him, honey. If anything can bring him back from the dead it's what you are doing here.' Outside he walked down to the Bonne Chance saloon. There was the usual night crowd there and the loud talk and noise. When he came in everything went quiet.

He could see Kelso at the bar, talking to Latour. He went over to them. He said, looking at Kelso and measuring his words, 'You killed a man who I figure could have finally beaten the bottle and become the man he had it in him to be. I can't touch you for it because it was supposed to be a fight he brought on. But he was a peace officer and I resent that very much.' He added slowly, 'But if I have occasion to come after you, Kelso, it will be through my own gunsmoke.'

He could feel the four eyes of the two men following him as he left and he knew they were smiling. But he knew, too, they had got the message and he was sure it was not sitting on them as lightly as they pretended.

NINE

Judge Archer was grim-faced. He stood in the marshal's office and stated his concern.

'This rustling, Martin – it's getting too big to be ignored. In this state and over the borders into both Nevada and Arizona Territory. There is a mighty big operation going on and everyone is pretty concerned, even the ranches that haven't been hit as yet.'

Sullivan agreed. 'That's about the size of it, Judge. But let me say there's a whole lot of thieves at work here. It's suggested that maybe the Palmer family is involved but that's only four men. There must be other riders and plenty of them. What is more, they cover a great deal of territory and they strike in entirely different places each time – now north, now south, now north-east, now south-west.'

The judge frowned. 'Yes, yes. I understand the difficulties involved but this is a near epidemic. God knows we've had rustlers at work ever since there's been a West but most have been driven off or shot or hanged. This time they seem to be doing as they please.' He looked squarely at Sullivan. 'Martin, I had you engaged because of your record as an honest, straight-shooting man who knew how to tame a town and keep things in order. But this hasn't got to do with drunken cowhands or dangerous gun-slingers. It's something else. Not beyond you, is it?'

Sullivan was silent a moment or two. He said slowly, 'Give me a little more time, Judge. I've got to find out exactly how they are working this. Where the cattle are driven to, who are the eventual buyers, why so many are needed.'

The judge grumbled, 'Meantime men are losing their cows worse than with the Texas fever. You had better get on with it, Martin. People are starting to wonder why the law isn't doing more.' He growled, 'We don't want ranchers riding the range with shot-guns and rifles. That could lead to all sorts of trouble, range feuds even and maybe innocent people getting shot.'

Sullivan said curtly, 'You realize I've had

one deputy shot dead and another disabled and possibly likely to die. That leaves a lot of ground for one man to cover.'

The judge said irritably, 'Appoint another couple of men – or even more. We've got to get this thing stopped.' He softened a little. 'That boy – will he live?'

'He's hanging on, Judge. He's a fighter. It's still nip and tuck but maybe the good Lord will take a hand.' The marshal flashed a keen glance at the other man. 'I'd say that your daughter is helping a lot. The doc says that Jerry somehow understands she is there and that it's a big factor in his possible recovery.'

The judge passed his hand a little worriedly through his sparse hair. 'Never known Faith to be so interested in any young feller before.' He drew himself up stiffly. 'Of course, it's an impossible situation. She can be friends with the boy if she cares to but anything further–' He waved a hand in dismissal.

He prepared to go on his way. He said abruptly, 'Good gritty thing that boy did in going after those cattle thieves. A little foolish maybe but with that sort of incentive he will surely make something of himself.' He added with a touch of genuine pity, 'If he survives, that is.'

Sullivan said soberly, 'He might just do that, Judge. Especially with your daughter so crazy keen to see that he does.' The judge frowned again and waved a hand in further touchy displeasure as he left.

Sullivan was thinking, it must be really something to have a woman so much worked up about whether a man lives or dies. He ran through in his mind the women he had known and smiled wryly. He couldn't imagine one of them weeping over his own possibly bullet-riddled corpse. Whatever eventually became of their interest in each other Jerry Owens and Faith Archer had stirred up something in one another that was eminently worthwhile.

That afternoon he rode out to the Slash C again. Even in the middle of all the troubles that had come upon him with Jim Moran's death, Jerry Owens' savage wounding and the high pressure being brought to bear upon him as an officer of the law to round up the rustlers, Theodora Cavendish still loomed largely in his thoughts.

He mused, the one woman he had met who drew him to her like the siren he had once heard of in school from a teacher fascinated by old Greek legends. As he rode he thought, what was her name? Something starting with a C and with her songs she lured passing sailors to her but they met their doom at her hands.

Well, yes, Theodora Cavendish sang with the same appeal and backed it up with a lush physical magnetism that could well in the long run be dangerous to any man. He consoled himself with the thought that he was a man wise in the ways of the world and especially its women flesh but there was a nagging notion in his mind that maybe –just maybe – there were hidden waters in this woman that he had as yet not plumbed.

That night she sang again, a certain melancholy in the sound.

'When I remember all
The friends, so linked together,
I've seen around me fall
Like leaves in wintry weather,
I feel like one
Who treads alone
Some banquet-hall deserted,
Whose lights are fled,
And garlands dead,
And all but he departed...'

She tinkled out the last notes on the piano.

Sullivan asked casually, 'You had something like that happen to you? Curly, maybe?'

She got up from the piano, smiling in the strange way that every now and then seemed to him so evasive, a dark woman's thoughts in a dark woman's head. She said, 'No, not Curly – not any man, really. It's maybe something that I feel sometimes I'll never have – a "he" that I feel that way about.'

Sullivan said shortly, 'Well, maybe I'm a substitute.'

She looked at him, her eyes suddenly glinting with a touch of caprice. 'And a very good substitute. Maybe the closest I'll ever get.'

Sullivan queried, 'What about Latour?'

She smiled. 'Too French. Too sure of himself as a lady-killer.' She was already sitting beside him, the loose gown she wore slowly sliding away from her. He ran his hand over her bare shoulders, the willing flesh exciting his brain. He picked her up and carried her from the room, her body limp and surrendered.

Later that night he was riding back to Estrada, the stars a chain of silver above him, the air soft and light. But somehow he felt a touch of shame, almost like a court favourite called now and then at a queen's bidding.

It was then the rifle spoke and the bullet flew past, almost near enough to have smashed his skull. He swung about in the saddle to look back, crouching down. Another shot followed, this time tearing the brim of his stetson.

He turned his horse about and headed in the direction of the marksman. He could hear a horse galloping away, its hoofs making the pattering sound of a cow pony. He stretched his big mount out, the huge black with the white blaze and the white socks. He knew that its long powerful strides that turned miles almost into yards would soon have him overtaking the fugitive rider.

The man did not shoot again. He was crouched over his pony, driving it furiously with quirt and spur. Sullivan stretched the black out to full speed. Its hooves were thundering now, beating the earth like drums, rapidly overtaking the runaway rider.

The man on the cow pony was pushing his mount too hard. Panting, its sides heaving, it suddenly stumbled and fell. The man, in the manner of an expert rider, threw himself clear. But at almost the same moment as he rolled over, his mount picking itself up and running on a few yards, Sullivan was out of the saddle and alongside the man, Smith & Wesson .44 in hand, the mouth of its bore a circle of black menace.

The man's hat had fallen off to show a mop of thick blond hair. He was big and muscular with the sort of brawny strength that came from roping, throwing and branding cows.

Sullivan said pleasantly, 'Ben Carson. Now, what's your quarrel with me – as if I didn't know. It's your boss lady, isn't it? You figure that I've taken your place with her – that my tin star has dazzled her and that I've stolen her out of your arms.'

The big blond-headed young man scowled. 'You're a lucky jasper I never got you with one of them shots.'

Sullivan corrected him. 'No, you're the lucky one. If you had hit me you would have been strung up for the murder of a peace officer.' He paused. 'I guess I can do one of two things. I can take you into custody and charge you with intent to murder. Or I can let you go and tell you to ride to hell and gone and never let me see you around here again.'

He said, thinking aloud, 'I guess I have been a mite provocative in your case.' He mused, 'I wonder just how many men your boss lady has set at one another's throats this way.'

Carson said doggedly. 'You ain't got no call to go talkin' 'bout her like that.'

'No. I guess I haven't. I figure she's been even more kindly to me than she's been to you.'

The foreman's eyes flashed red anger. 'You wouldn't talk so big if you wasn't holdin' a gun on me.'

Sullivan considered for a moment. Then he dropped the gun to the ground. He said quietly, 'That better? Now, what do you figure on doing?'

The bulky young foreman, a sudden look of triumph in his eyes, lunged forward, fists raised. He had beaten up more than his share of cowpunchers in saloons and in bunkhouse quarrels. But when he got to Sullivan the marshal wasn't there. He had moved backwards on quick, sure feet, hands coming up in the easy relaxed stance of the practised fist-fighter.

Carson, grunting, moved forward again, fists swinging. Sullivan stepped in close, easily avoiding the wild blows. His left fist suddenly rammed into the foreman's middle with the force of a pole driven into the flesh. Immediately his right fist cracked against

Carson's jaw, hard bone bruising bone.

The foreman staggered, breath gone, mouth flying open. Sullivan hit him again with two fierce hooks, one left, one right, both to the sagging jaw. Carson went down, beaten, winded, heavily bruised, lucky not to have his jaw broken.

Sullivan looked down at him. He said calmly, 'Let's quit this foolishness before I do you some damage. When you've got some breath back I want to ask you a few questions.' Carson sat up, groaning a little and then got up very slowly, hands feeling his jaw cautiously.

Sullivan said conversationally, 'Been a lot of rustling going on. Your boss know anything about it? I hear tell that some of your outfit seem to go missing now and then and that your boss has fired what were good men to hire some others – drifters with a no-good look about them.'

He stopped and waited. Painfully Carson walked over and picked up his hat. He put it on and made for his horse.

Sullivan called, 'Chatterbox, aren't you? Well, maybe it isn't too easy to talk with that jaw.' He raised his voice. 'Remember what I said, Carson. Get out of Estrada, this area, pronto. If I see you around any more I'll come after you not with fists but with a gun. And I'll make you wish your two shots had not missed.'

The foreman climbed up on his pony and rode off without another word. Sullivan watched him go. He guessed he would not see the man again. Carson didn't want to be arrested and he could see that his favoured position with Theodora Cavendish was over. He would leave.

Sullivan sighed a little. The foreman had not proved to be any help, information wise, but his silence had indicated he knew things he didn't want to talk about. The marshal got up on the big black and headed for town.

The next afternoon he made one of his regular visits to see how things were with Jerry Owens. When we went in he got the immediate feeling that something had happened.

The doctor met him with a grin. 'That boy of yours – good news. He's breathing like a baby. I would say he is close to turning the corner. Incredible. Got a husky young frame, of course, but that girl–' He wagged his head.

'I tell you, Marshal, there is really something to that thing they call thought transference. She has been willing him to get better and his thoughts have been responding to hers and, by Jupiter, he's on the road back.'

Sullivan, the ice in his eyes again thawing at the words, went in to the boy's bedside. Faith was not there. He guessed she must sleep sometime. But as he looked at the youth he saw the difference. The strain, the tiredness, the death look was gone and Jerry was sleeping quietly, every sign about him of someone who had crossed the borderland into beyond and yet had somehow been drawn back. He figured the girl had willed him back.

He tiptoed out. Well, the kid would still need a lot of nursing but he was going to live. Sullivan felt a glow about that. No child of his own, he knew now that what he had always felt for this boy – even when he had sent him out on foot into that bleak desert area – was a fatherly feeling. He guessed he had better go and share the good news with the girl.

The judge nodded, pleased. 'Glad to hear it. It would have been a bad thing if he had died after being shot down by a cowardly rustler.'

Mrs Archer sniffed. 'Yes, well, John Freeman is an excellent doctor. I'm sure he did a lot to bring this about.'

Sullivan said clearly, 'Not as much as your daughter. Doc Freeman told me it was she who really willed the boy to get better.'

Miriam Archer looked startled. 'Stuff and nonsense! Good doctoring did it, that's all.'

Faith looked across at Sullivan, her eyes conveying appreciation and understanding of what he had said. Her voice was quiet. 'I'm so very, very glad. But he'll need a lot of nursing yet. And I intend to help all I can.' Her parents exchanged disapproving glances but Sullivan knew this was a girl with a will of iron who would do what she said. He thought again with a slight stab of loneliness how he envied the boy.

The judge asked sharply, 'Any nearer to rounding up those rustlers?'

Sullivan said soberly, 'Closer, Judge, closer. But it's not going to be easy.' He thought with a hollow feeling that if Theodora Cavendish was really involved there was going to be some real hurt in it for himself.

As he left, the marshal was wondering if he was ever going to find a woman who would be to him what Faith Archer was to his young deputy. As he hung up his gunbelt that night he looked at it and thought, my one true friend. But it could never take the place of a truly loving woman.

TEN

Jerry Owens got up slowly and walked across the room. He was like an old man riddled with sciatica and dreading each step.

Faith, eyes shining, burst out, 'Fine, that's just fine! Bravo!'

Jerry turned back towards the bed, eyeing it like some earnestly desired haven. He puffed, 'Not real easy. Gosh, seems like they put someone else's legs on me.'

Faith went to his side and put an arm around his shoulders. He felt her against him, warm and soft and yet strong. He was so very glad she was there. She said encouragingly, 'That's good, that's really good. But you mustn't try too hard just yet. A little at a time.' She helped him to the bed and he sank back on it gratefully.

She sat down alongside him. She said earnestly, 'You know, Jerry, you're going to need a good bit of help yet. You can't stay here indefinitely.' She set her mouth. 'I'm going to get you home with me.'

He stared, mouth slightly agape. 'But your

folks – they wouldn't–'

She said firmly, 'My folks are good, honest, kind people. Oh, they fuss and carry on about me and my–' she smiled – 'wilful ways but they always come around to doing what is right and generous and decent.'

The boy sat up a little and gasped with the effort. 'But, Faith, your dad wouldn't–'

She brushed him aside. 'My dad is rough and grumpy and talks loudly but you won't find a kinder man anywhere. You are coming home with us and staying until you are really well again and there's an end of it.'

She propped him up on the pillows. 'So there, Mister Deputy Jerome Owens. You'll just have to like it.'

He gazed at her, his eyes reflecting her own warmth of feeling. 'Like it? Like it? Why, "like" just ain't the word.'

She scolded him. 'Now, there's something. There's no such word as ain't. I'm sure your mother told you that.'

'Well, yes, but sometimes it just slips out.'

Faith smiled. 'That's the one concession you'll have to make to fit in with our family. Don't say ain't. Not a hard one to keep, is it, now?'

He grinned up at her. 'No, it ain't – uh – it is not.' Faith on a sudden impulse bent down and kissed him. He sank back on the pillows, hardly believing it had happened. The healing of Jerry Owens was well on the way.

Sullivan had been out riding far and wide. Slowly he was beginning to piece things together. The picture wasn't really clear as yet but it was emerging bit by bit.

He got down off the big black horse and studied the tracks again. He had followed them now for miles and they were clearly heading south for the border. He knew the terrain and he knew also that on the trail they were taking they would strike water holes and grazing spots. It was a lot of beef on the hoof and they would need all that to get the cows to their destination in reasonable condition.

But why weren't they headed east for the railheads, for Dodge? They could do the rebranding but evidently they were not bothering about that. Whoever the buyers were they didn't give a damn about brands.

That suggested that a lot of the cows were due for an early demise and soon to enter the throats of the hungry buyers at the end of the drive. But where and who?

Sullivan got back on his horse and headed

home. It would take him a while to get there. This was a big operation and trying to track it down had led him a long way from Estrada but a night or two at a lonely campfire would give him time to think, to try to come to some conclusions. He rode on, the big horse's slow even tread helping his thoughts.

He leaned forward and patted the stock of the rifle in his saddle boot and then let his hand slip comfortably over the butt of the .44 strapped to his side. He may need them in a hurry if the rustlers thought he was getting a mite too curious.

He pushed on, with a mental note to maybe make cold camp that night.

When Sullivan got back he left the tired big black at the livery and walked wearily back to his office.

He was surprised to find a woman waiting for him. It was Sadie Torrence, his landlady. She said brusquely, 'You look plumb tired, Marshal. Been out ridin', I see.'

Sullivan met her on the boardwalk. 'Yes, ma'am, and not just for pleasure along some bridle path like the rich folks do.'

She surveyed him keenly. 'Yeah. I figger there ain't much you do for pleasure, Marshal. Unless, of course, it has to do with Miz Cavendish.'

He gave her a cold stare. 'You wanted to see me about something?'

The big-bosomed woman nodded. 'Sure did, Marshal. It's an invite.'

He stared. 'An invitation?'

'Yup. I'm gittin' together what you might call a little dinner party. You have been absent for a day or two, out on a trail by the looks of you, an' I guarantee you are feelin' like some good grub instead of that hard tack you been chompin' on.'

Sullivan relaxed. 'Well, I find your vittles at all times mighty tasty, ma'am, and I'm sure that if you are putting on something special it will be just that. I'd be very pleased to be there.' He eyed her curiously. 'And who, might I ask, are the other guests?'

She said briefly, 'You'll find out. Won't be too many. Jest cosy like. See you in my private rooms tomorrow night then, about supper time.' She walked off, her big hips swinging a little as she moved.

Sullivan watching her could see that she had not been exactly the ugliest saloon girl around when she had followed that trade years ago. He smiled a little. In many ways, she was an intriguing woman. He felt interested in what tomorrow night might bring.

In the afternoon he decided to go along

and see how Jerry Owens was faring. The doctor met him, smiling. 'Gone. Faith Archer took him home. Said she could handle the nursing better there. Don't doubt but what that feisty girl can.'

Sullivan was taken aback. 'But the judge and Mrs Archer–'

The doctor grinned. 'That girl could talk Satan into turning hell into a comfortable rest home for the aged. The judge and Mrs Archer are no match for her. The boy's home with them now, getting fed like a turkey cock, no doubt, and lying back on pillows trimmed with lace.'

Sullivan grinned slowly in turn. He said wistfully, 'With a girl like that the boy can't fail to make it in the world. Guess I'll get along to see him.'

At the Archers' place the judge gave a grimace. 'Well, it was not our idea – that is, Miriam and me – but Faith talks so hard and she has always been one to look out for lame dogs and cats and the like.' He paused. 'Anyway, the boy is here and I guess it's good to see he is much on the improve.'

Sullivan gave a wisp of a smile. 'Of course, she would have to have inherited a lot of that from somewhere. Any idea, Judge?'

Judge Archer coughed. 'Ah, yes, well–' He

changed the subject. 'About those rustlers.'

Sullivan's eyes narrowed, the ice creeping back. 'I'm finding out a few things. It looks to me like the thieves are heading for one big bang-up sale fetching many thousands of dollars. But just where and to whom I haven't quite figured out as yet.'

The judge studied him appraisingly. He said abruptly, 'You have a big supporter in that boy. I spoke to him a trifle critically about your failure so far to get on to these thieves and, for all his weakness, he came back at me like a mountain lion stung by a flesh wound. He knows what the word loyalty means.'

The marshal nodded acknowledgment. 'If I had had a son I would have settled for one like him.'

The judge surveyed him shrewdly. 'Not too late for that yet, Martin. Why don't you find yourself a bride? You must have met a lot of women.'

'That's true, Judge. But they all seemed just a little too grasping, what you would call acquisitive, if you know what I mean.' His eyes clouded over with a touch of melancholy. He said dispiritedly, 'Even the ones who sometimes draw you to them the most.'

The judge shrugged. 'Take my tip, Martin,

no man's life is complete without a good woman in it. Now, my Miriam is not perfect but I tell you I would be only half a man without her.'

'I get your drift, Judge, but just count me among the unlucky ones.' He said briskly, 'I'll go see the boy and then I've got other business to attend to.'

Later, the other business took the marshal down to the Bonne Chance saloon. He somehow had the idea that if there was anything crooked and yet highly profitable on anyone's agenda Eugene Latour would have a strong chance of being included.

When he entered the saloon he spotted Latour sitting at a table at the far end. The man he was talking to was Gil Kelso.

Sullivan walked up to them. Kelso looked up at him, cool and dapper, voice as expressionless as that of an undertaker. 'Howdy, Marshal.' He slowly put his hand down to the gun on his hip and laid it carefully on the table. 'Take a look at it. Ain't been fired recently. Anyway, mostly it's aimed at coyotes and rattlers.'

Sullivan queried, 'You don't really get around to shooting your own kind like that, do you, Kelso?'

The gunman's eyes took on even more the

dull, blank look of the killer. 'Now, that ain't a real nice thing to say, Marshal.'

Latour broke in, smiling at Sullivan. 'A drink, *mon ami?*'

Sullivan shook his head. 'No, thanks. I admire your hospitality but this isn't really a courtesy call.'

Latour raised an eyebrow. 'Really, *m'sieur?* What is the occasion?'

'Well, now, I hate to bring this up, you understand, but there's been an awful lot of rustling going on lately and I am making enquiries all over.'

Latour's smile widened. He spread delicately manicured hands. 'I sell liquor and supply gambling devices for the use of men hungry for both. That only.'

The marshal prompted, 'And girls to go with it.'

Latour pursed his lips. 'The girls are around. What they and our clients do together is their business.' He raised his upper lip at one corner. 'With the exception, you may have noted, of our star attraction, the one known as The Kansas Sunflower. She is what one might call, ah, virginal.'

Sullivan said softly, 'Given up trying to get her to change her mind?' Latour gave a silent shrug. The marshal went on. 'I just want to say that I am going to catch these rustlers cold and see they get what is coming to them.'

Kelso's voice was as cold as the ice in the marshal's eyes. 'That might lead to some dangerous shooting. Think you can handle that?'

Sullivan said evenly, 'Even if your own gun is doing some of the shooting, yes, I still figure I can handle it.'

Kelso carefully returned his weapon to its holster. He was smiling now. It was something like a death's head trying to pretend it had flesh covering it.

'I am a peaceable man, Marshal. That is, until someone happens to rile me real bad. Then I sort of lose the urge not to disturb the peace.'

Sullivan took them both in with a long searching look. 'Just a word, gentlemen. Stick to selling liquor, supplying decks of cards and–' he flicked a crisp glance at Kelso – 'being peaceable. It will pay in the long run.'

As he walked away he knew there were two pairs of eyes following him that were far from friendly. But he had not come to make friends, he had come to warn them. He hoped the warning had had some effect. But he knew that Gil Kelso had been warned before and had killed the men who had warned him. He hoped that he would not have to try to reverse that through gun-smoke. But if it happened it happened. He thought wryly, both marshals and gunmen came and went but life went on.

Later that day he knocked on the door of one of the couple of rooms in the lodging-house Sadie Torrence reserved for herself. It opened immediately. Sullivan gaped. The big buxom woman was dressed in a red satin gown that showed off the fullness of a figure he decided then must have had the cowhands whooping when she had been a saloon girl.

She said impatiently, 'Well, don't jest stand there gawking. Come on in.' Sullivan stepped inside and was immediately aware of another presence. Once again his eyes flickered a little at the sight. It was Lilian Blainey, The Kansas Sunflower of the Bonne Chance.

Sullivan seemed to be taking her in for the first time. She was not dressed in the same flamboyant manner as Sadie Torrence but everything she wore enhanced the depth of the beauty he had not really observed before.

She had on a clean-cut gown that showed off what he realized was her splendid figure and her hair was falling down her back in a golden stream held by a velvet ribbon at the back of her head. She looked like a picture he had once seen of some blonde beauty of ancient legend.

She stared at him almost with shock. Sadie Torrence planted herself alongside them. She urged, 'That's it. Take a good look at each other 'cause this is all the company you're gunna see here tonight.' She gestured to the girl. 'See this here man? He ain't a woman-hatin', man-killin' demon like you mighta figgered him for.'

She nodded at the girl. 'Take a good look at this woman. She ain't no painted-up, slick-fingered harpy lookin' to give you the come-on an' then rob you blind. She is a beautiful girl, earnin' a honest livin'.'

She looked around her. 'I think we got somethin' kinda cosy here tonight. An' I figger we all ought to git to know each other better over this here meal I cooked up. Jest you two sit here while I git it...'

Afterwards, walking the blonde back to the Bonne Chance for her nightly perform-ances Sullivan was silent. She broke in on his thoughts. 'Well, Marshal, you have a most unusual landlady.'

Sullivan stopped on the boardwalk and looked at her candidly. 'Yes, I have and that's the truth.' He hesitated a moment. 'I want to offer you an apology for anything I ever said that might have offended you.'

She was silent in turn. She put out a finely-shaped gloved hand. 'And I, too, Marshal. I'm afraid I was a little astray in my own judgement.'

When they reached the Bonne Chance they stood outside for a moment. A couple of passers-by gave them a curious look and went on, whispering to each other and glancing back at them. She said suddenly, 'Do you think that Mrs Torrence's idea in arranging this little tête-à-tête was just to assure us both that the other person was not all that – ah – unattractive as we thought?'

Sullivan shook his head. 'No, I don't think that was all she had in mind at all.'

She smiled suddenly. 'Nor do I, Marshal. Nor do I.' As she went in to the saloon he turned to go. Somehow the dark beauty of Theodora Cavendish had begun to have a slightly less compelling allure.

ELEVEN

Sullivan was about to lock up and to leave his office at the jailhouse when the door opened and she came in.

He gave her a surprised glance. He wondered then why he had taken so long to notice that the gold in her hair owed nothing to bleaching. It was, he thought, as pure and unadulterated as the sunlight. An accompanying thought was that this woman had other qualities, too, that were just as authentic.

Lilian Blainey was not smiling. He sensed she had come with something he needed to know. He gestured her to a chair. She sat up, straight backed and graceful, every line of her etched with an easy openness. He could not help but compare it with the dark, often unapproachable mystery of Theodora Cavendish.

She said soberly, 'I've come to tell you something you may not like.'

Sullivan eased himself down into a chair behind his desk. 'Been told a lot of things I didn't like. Gotten used to it.'

She studied him quietly. 'This gets to be very personal.'

'Oh.' He spread his hands. 'I've learned to handle that, too.'

She went on, unhurried but clear and precise. 'You know that Eugene Latour has a sort of, well, fancy for me. You'll recall how you one time–'

'Busted up his rough approach,' contributed Sullivan. 'He been at it again?'

'Well, not in the same way. But he's been trying to win me over in other ways. With gifts and all sorts of small courtesies. A sort of refined French way.'

Sullivan's mouth gave a suggestion of a smile. 'Go on.'

The girl's sober look did not change. 'So much so that he's taken me into his confidence about several things.' She paused a moment. 'He came to my dressing-room the other night and talked a lot – a very great deal, as a matter of fact. He was as near drunk as he ever gets and he said some things that he may have regretted later. Really, it was all in an attempt to win me over.' She stopped for a moment and then went on.

'Latour told me that he has a big project under way that will bring him in thousands of dollars. He told me that if I was what he called co-operative he would be prepared to share it with me. He talked about selling up the saloon and going to New Orleans or New York and even overseas. With me as his companion, of course.'

Sullivan asked, 'What is this project?'

'It seems to have to do with cattle.'

Sullivan sat up in his chair. 'Rustled cattle?'

She stared. 'Perhaps.'

He asked slowly, 'Anyone else with him in this?'

She wrinkled her brow. 'It seems that Theodora Cavendish has been a sort of silent partner with him in a few things. But it also appears they are coming to the end of the road as partners.' She gave him a long look. 'I gather they have been lovers but Theodora appears to have a new romantic interest. He made a point of telling me this to assure me that I had no rival for his so-called affections.'

Sullivan got up and took a few steps across the room. He turned slowly to face her. He spoke her name for the first time. 'Lilian, what you've told me is very important. I thank you for it.' He went on briskly. 'Don't let Latour know anything about your coming to me with this.' He threw a question at her. 'How do you feel about staying on at the Bonne Chance?'

She shrugged. 'I'm being paid well and I've handled over-amorous employers before.'

Sullivan moved back to her. He leaned down and said urgently, 'It would suit me if you could pass on to me anything else like this you hear. You've got that deadly little pea-shooter. Use it on him if you really have to and there'll be no complaints from the law.'

He leaned a little closer and kissed her on the lips. She remained still. Then she reached up and touched him gently on the cheek with the tips of her fingers. She stood up and moved over to the door. Then looked back. Her voice held a little disturbed enquiry. 'That woman – are you and she–'

Sullivan said, 'Put it this way. The fair queen of hearts has always appealed to me more than the dark queen of spades.' She smiled slowly as she left. Sullivan went down to the livery for the big black horse he called Ace. He was headed for the Slash C.

Theodora, he considered, had rarely looked more seductive. The flowing tea-gown she wore seemed almost part of her sensuous flesh. She asked blankly, 'What on earth are you talking about?'

Sullivan stood straddle-legged and upright, the law incarnate, strong and unmoving. 'I've told you – don't meddle any further with this. You are liable to get into really big trouble. I could do more to you but right now I'm simply warning you. Pull out before it's too late.'

She moved away from him, angry in her dark, brooding way. 'This is all nonsense – me involved in a rustling activity–'

He said patiently, 'I've tracked sign all over. You have fired good riders and hired no-good saddle-tramps. They seem to be away from the Slash C more than they are here. I heard from someone that you and Latour were seen in the company of the Palmer boys even after that ruckus at the Bonne Chance. And it appears the Palmers have a ranch they rarely seem to be at.'

He added, 'I've also been in touch with law officers in New Orleans and they tell me Latour has as bad a reputation as any no-good gambler in the city.'

She was silent. She turned to face him. She said coldly, 'All supposition.'

'Maybe. But when you add one thing to another the supposition begins to look mighty like fact.'

She brushed a long strand of ebony hair back from the dark-skinned perfection of her face. 'So you've come out to give me a warning? What made you bother to do that?'

He faced her directly. 'You and I have been – close. Physically, that is. Not any other way because, speaking candidly, Theodora, that's all you have to give. Every other way you are no man's woman. But I thought I owed you something for a few pleasurable evenings.'

She lowered her lids a little down over the amber pools of her eyes. 'They are still available.'

'No, Theodora. Our little affair has come to the stage of *adios*, farewell and goodbye. But I would like to think that you have had the sense to back off from what could have very nasty consequences for you.'

After he had gone she stood frowning. Then she went quickly into another room and changed speedily into riding clothes. She called a passing cowhand, slouch-shouldered and unshaven, part of her new crew, to get her a horse. When it came she mounted and headed for a line hut on her range.

Reaching it she dismounted and called out. A tousled blond head showed itself as

Ben Carson opened the door for her.

As she went in she stared at him contemptuously. 'Why I keep you skulking around here I'll never know.' She shot him a look of disdain. 'You know, of course, that if Sullivan sees you he'll put a bullet through your hide.'

He said sullenly, 'Not if I see him first.'

She flared, 'Like the last time, eh? You appear to have had him dead to rights and you couldn't hit him even then.' She said irritably, 'You'll have to leave here and go some place else to hide.'

He held out his hands, suddenly pleading like a child. 'Don't send me away. You know I'm crazy about you – always will be. I ain't sure I can keep on livin' if you turn me out. Lemme jest be around you–'

She curled her lip. 'Stop your blubbering.' She eyed him viciously. 'You know all that was on your side, don't you? You were just someone for me to pass the time with for a while.'

He was down on his knees now, begging her. He was a man utterly in the grip of a dominant woman. She looked down at him scornfully. 'There's been other men – there always will be. There was Eugene Latour–'

A sudden gleam came into her eyes, a

144

thought that had taken hold of her enigmatic mind. She said deliberately, 'Of course, you know all about Eugene and how we've been engaged on his little enterprise together – you've ridden for us on it.' She stood back and stared at him, her dark eyes suddenly melting and working their hypnosis on him. Her voice had become soft and warm. 'You've no reason to like Eugene, have you, Ben? You know that I preferred him to you as a lover. But here's a chance for you to change that.' Her voice became winning, subtle. 'In my arrangement with Latour we split fifty-fifty. But one hundred percent always seems to me to be much more agreeable.'

Her eyes had become plainly alluring with a touch of mesmerism. 'If there was no Eugene I would be the sole organizer and the sole profiteer.' She moved nearer to him and touched his unshaven cheek caressingly with the back of her hand. 'Maybe then you and I...'

He looked at her with the eyes of a dog ready to comply with his mistress's slightest command. 'You mean that you an' me – if I go after the Frenchie...?'

She nodded, her eyes holding his steadily with a stare like that of a sorceress willing a hireling to do her bidding. He grabbed her hand and kissed it. 'Theodora, so help me, I'll do it. I'll git him dead to rights, that Frenchman with his perfume an' fancy clothes...' His not-so-bright face was suddenly convulsed with hate. 'When I think of the times he's had his hands on you—'

She stepped back from him, slowly disengaging his grip. 'Keep thinking of it, Ben. It'll help you to do it. And keep thinking of you and me and what we could do together when all those rustled cows are sold.'

She blew him a kiss from the door. She almost whispered, 'As I recall, your arms were stronger and even more demanding than Eugene's. I liked that.'

When she had gone he moved quickly to the gunbelt and strapped it on. He thought, it would need to be at night and done fast. He didn't want to run into the marshal. Not that, he convinced himself, he was afraid of him but there was something in Sullivan's eyes that told of a complete ruthlessness whenever the lawman decided to take a hand in something that stirred him up.

Ben Carson shivered just a little but then turned his thoughts back to Eugene Latour. It was more comforting. The former ramrod of the Slash C had ridden many trails in his young life, one including the owlhoot. Killing a man was not an imponderable thought nor an act strange to his hand.

And the big thing about it was that Theodora would again be his. He would ride into Estrada that very night.

Ben Carson moved through the shadows in a way not entirely foreign to him. He was lurking near the Bonne Chance, looking for an opportunity to spot Latour and to catch him alone. He did not know where it would be – inside, outside, wherever.

He was counting on the unexpectedness of the attack, coming out of the dark, and the rapidity of his own getaway with his horse hitched up at a nearby rail.

He had been edging about the saloon for about an hour or so now and although he had once or twice glimpsed the Frenchman through the swing doors as customers had both entered and emerged he had not as yet got anything like a chance at a clear shot.

He was sneaking up to the back of the saloon, making up his mind to gain a silent entry that way, when a voice pulled him up in his tracks. It was quiet with a queer tonelessness in it but it had the kind of threat that needed to be listened to.

'I been keepin' an eye on you since you started your prowlin', stranger. You appear to be up to somethin' that you might call no-good. Otherwise you wouldn't be creepin' around like a coyote around a henhouse.' The voice added informatively, 'You see, man, the boss of this here saloon hires me to sort of watch out for him. Which I been doin'. Turn around slow. Hands away from that pistol you are carryin'.'

Ben Carson twisted slowly around to face the owner of the voice. Gil Kelso stared at him. 'Hey, you are somethin' to do with the Slash C, ain't you? Let's take a little walk, you an' me, an' we'll figger this out. I guess the boss will be interested.'

Ben Carson noted that the gunman did not have a pistol in his hand. He went for his own weapon. He had drawn it before the other man moved and was making for his horse at the same time, intending to keep Kelso covered while he made his escape.

But even as he pointed his weapon warningly at the other man Kelso in an almost invisible movement drew and fired. Ben Carson reeled back, his own finger involuntarily pulling the trigger in a sort of reflex twitch. His shot went into the air as he crumpled down beside the nervous hoofs of his horse to lie there, motionless in death.

When the marshal came and a small crowd had gathered, Kelso said easily, 'A prowler I caught movin' around. Asked him what he was doin' an' he pulled a gun on me. I shot in self-defence.'

Sullivan mused, 'You appear to be an awful set-upon man.' He ran his eyes over the gunman. 'I see his shot got nowhere near you.'

Kelso shrugged. 'Jest a natural bad shot, Marshal.' He drawled, 'For which I am right glad.'

'Yes. Well, there's no one around to say different, Kelso, so it looks like you are in the clear again. But I would advise you to keep that weapon of yours closer to your holster than your hand. It seems that every time you draw it someone gets killed.'

The gunman shrugged and walked away. Later, Sullivan thought it over. Theodora must have been harbouring him. And then to come into town and start hanging around outside the Bonne Chance at night. To do the Frenchman harm? If so, had it been at his own urging or at Theodora's instructions?

He hoped the latter. When thieves fell out they were easier to catch.

But as he went to bed he sighed. There was a long way to go before the actual catching took place.

TWELVE

Big Rube Palmer rubbed his jaw. He said reflectively, 'The way I see it we do all the work an' run all the risks. Why shouldn't we git the big profits?'

His three brothers sat around like a trio of shaggy barbarians, rough half beards and hair long and tangled. The oldest of the three, Jess, spoke up.

'Reckon you're right, big Brother.' His eyes took on the lustful look of a satyr. He licked lips as thick and greasy as sausages freshly fried. 'What I couldn't do with all that money among them whirlago girls in 'Frisco.'

Big Rube reminded him, 'Ain't got it yet, Brother. But I figger we ought to aim to.' The other two nodded slowly. 'Yup, we is with you, Brother.'

The youngest one, Sammy, nodded vigorously. 'Like you said, Reuben, we is the ones takin' all the chances. Maybe some crazy rancher gunna come close to puttin' a load of buckshot in our hide one day.'

The huge elder brother got to his feet. He belched loudly and looked accusingly at his younger brother. 'Git our right earnin's an' we won't need to keep spendin' money on bicarbonate to give us some ease after downin' the chow Sammy here serves up to us.'

Sammy scowled. Big Rube yawned. He said with a tone of finality, 'Well, it's settled then. Before we pull out in the mornin' I'll go see that Mex colonel.' They spread out their bedrolls and went to sleep, like four hogs sprawling in a pen.

Colonel Anastasio Roque de la Huerta was a slim man with a scarred face and eyes like a wolf peering from behind cover. He had ambition big enough to envision himself sitting in a chair sufficiently large to contain the president of all Mexico. He also had a rebel army that required feeding. He was prepared to buy rustled beef from across the border with no questions asked.

He received the giant in his tent with a frown. This fat gringo was not his idea of a gentleman but then Americans generally were a barbaric race. He snapped, 'You wanted to speak with me. What is it?'

Big Rube jerked out, 'You payin' Horton twenty dollars a head for them cows, aincha?'

'That is so.'

'How'd ya like to have 'em fer fifteen a head?'

The colonel stared. 'What do you mean?'

Big Rube leered, 'That's the price – if you pay me instead of Horton.'

The colonel narrowed his eyes. So, the gringos were not above cheating each other. As a past master himself at the art, he admired anyone who could do a really sharp deal. He smiled. 'I think I understand you, *mi amigo*. But what of Señor Horton?'

Big Rube leered again. 'He won't be no trouble. Me an' my brothers will see to that. If you pay us instead of Horton you'll git your beeves fer fifteen dollars a head.'

The colonel inquired shrewdly, 'What of the other men engaged?'

Big Rube grinned. 'The ones from the Slash C an' the others that Horton's own boss, Latour, hired for the rustlin'? They'll still git their cut. A mite less but we brothers don't figger they'll complain. If they do they'll need to be mighty quick on the draw.'

The colonel hesitated slightly and then

put out his hand. 'A deal, *señor.*' He winced as the big man crunched his hand in a bone-bending grip.

After Rube Palmer had gone, the colonel thought a while. And then a rat-like gleam came into his eyes. Why not let Horton know abut this and pass it on to Latour? If the thieves could have a real falling out and take to gunning each other down he could collect the entire herd for nothing. He would bide his time and move in with his troops when the rustlers' animosity towards each other was at its height. He already had a couple of his men stationed permanently on the Horton ranch until the full quota of beef was gathered.

He smiled at his own cunning. Yes, he would make a scheming overlord fit for the leadership of the whole Mexican nation.

Jerry Owens was starting to move about freely. He no longer needed to depend upon Faith's arm and firm shoulders to support him. He regretted that in a way. The fresh fragrance of the girl so close to him had been a very distinct pleasure.

As he sat up at the meal table he burst out, 'Well, Judge, sir, and Mrs Archer, ma'am, I want to thank you for the keen way you have given me your hospitality and been so very kind. I guess I'll always remember. You have been like loving parents to me.'

The judge harrumphed, 'Nonsense, boy. Thank Faith. She's the one who's done it all.'

Miriam Archer had loosened up. She looked across the table at the boy and there was a touch of cordiality in her smile.

'We appreciate the way you have behaved with us, Jerome. Your mother taught you well.'

Jerry smiled back at her. 'So did my pa. They are the best of folks. But,' he added hastily, 'you sure do match them.'

Miriam Archer preened herself a little. 'Some more coffee, Jerome?'

He nodded, swallowing a trifle hard at his dislike of the use of his full name but knowing that if their improved relationship was to continue it was something he would have to bear.

'Thank you, ma'am. Your coffee is purely fine tasting.' The judge's wife preened herself a little more as she handed him another steaming cup.

The judge asked suddenly, 'What do you intend to do now, lad?'

Jerry gave him a surprised look. 'Why, go

back to my deputizing for the marshal.'

'Son, that is not the most danger-free occupation to be found. There must be something else for you with a less hazardous future to it.' He ran his eyes over Jerry. 'You are young enough to learn something else that could be of greater advantage to you.'

The boy said hotly, 'Marshal Sullivan is a fine man. There ain't any shame in wanting to be like him.'

Faith, smiling, murmured, 'You said ain't again, Jerry.'

''Cos I'm a little riled up, that's all.'

The judge said soberly, 'When it's all boiled down, fine man and all that he is, Martin Sullivan lives by the sword. I think we might be able to point you in a better direction.'

After he had packed his few things together on leaving again for his lodging-house, Jerry walked to the gate with Faith. He said earnestly, 'I'm really sorry for getting a little riled up at the table with your pa. Your ma and pa are good folks. But I sort of look up to the marshal.'

'I know you do, Jerry, and that's fine because he took you in and put you on the right track. But I still think you ought to listen to the judge in regard to your future.

He is a wise man.'

Jerry shook his head. 'I dunno, Faith. I'm set on being a good lawman.'

Faith smiled. 'Well, there are many sides to the law. We'll see.' As he went off he wondered a moment just what she had meant. But, he reassured himself, a marshal's badge was what he was looking for. He headed for his lodging-house with the good feeling that at least Faith's parents were now tolerant of him.

Latour called Kelso in. He said shortly, 'Sit down. We must talk.' The gunslinger eased himself into a chair, a question mark behind his expressionless gaze.

The Frenchman said testily, 'We have a problem. Those Palmers–'

Kelso said easily, 'Not surprised. They are a troublesome family.'

Latour nodded. *'Oui.* I have received information from Colonel de la Huerta that Big Rube is attempting a double-cross. He has offered to sell the herd cheaper to the Mexicans so long as he is paid the money.'

A faint flicker of a grin twitched the gunman's face. 'Uh-huh. And you plan to do something about it?'

'Not precisely, *mon ami.* I want *you* to do

something about it.' He continued irritably, 'We cannot have an outright – how do you say? – showdown over this right now. It would upset our plans and we are close to having a full herd ready for the sale.'

He took a cheroot from a box on his desk and handed the gunman another. They lit up together. Latour blew out some smoke. He said deliberately, 'I want you to teach them a lesson. A very severe one. We don't want to dispense with their services entirely but just to bring them to hand. You understand me?'

Kelso surveyed the end of his cheroot. His grin was that of a carnivore that had just feasted on one easy prey but was prepared to go immediately after another because of an insatiable lust for blood.

'Got you.' He came to his feet. 'I'll hit the trail today.'

Latour thought, I wish all my problems were solved so easily. That weapon of his is a mighty persuader.

The dark figure came from the shadows like some sinister genie conjured up out of the night. This time he was wearing two guns strapped to his thighs, weapons of death.

The four brothers squatted around the

campfire stared blankly. He had come up on them so silently they had not heard a twig snap or the slightest chink of a stone.

Kelso said softly, 'Evenin', boys. Don't bother offerin' me coffee. I ain't plannin' to stay long.'

One of the brothers, sensing the possible ominous nature of the visit, sneaked his hand towards his revolver. Kelso's voice had the usual cold tone, making one think of a corpse raising its head to speak from a coffin.

'Don't do that. I can have my pistol out and put a slug in your guts before you can git your fingers around that thing.'

The brother relaxed and drew his hand back. Kelso went on conversationally, 'I got a quarrel with only one of you. The rest of you stay out of it.' He fixed his gaze directly on Big Rube. 'I hear it was your idea to double-cross my boss. You're the one I've come to see.'

Big Rube leaned his bulk forward, squinting. He said urgently, 'You can be in on it, Kelso. It's fine pickins. You can come in with us.'

The gunman said in the same calm voice, 'Thanks, big feller, but no, thanks. Latour pays me pretty right and I ain't bankin' on gittin' into any double-dealin' like this. There could be all kinds of hitches, 'specially with them treacherous greasers involved.' His voice grew even flatter. 'I'll trouble you to stand up, big feller. You got a gun on your hip, I see. Let's see how fast you can git it out.'

Big Rube lumbered slowly to his feet. 'Now, look here, Kelso–'

The other three sat still, awed into silence by the figure of lethal judgment standing before them.

'I'm lookin', fat man.'

Big Rube with a movement of total desperation went for his gun. There were four shots following each other with almost the sound of one. Kelso had a gun in each hand with wisps of smoke coming out of the barrels.

Big Rube, his chest a mass of holes through which blood was already seeping, his hand empty of the gun it had been grasping for, toppled headfirst into the fire.

Kelso's cold voice rasped, 'Pull him out unless you want him roasted like a turkey.'

One of the brothers grabbed the body and dragged it back. Kelso said in the same dead tone, 'Jest you other three boys keep on rustlin' like you was paid to do. Put the loss

of your big brother there down to careless-
ness.'

He stepped back into the shadows. The
three men, still shaking from the thunder-
flash of the advent, stumbled around to
carry the limp weight of the giant away to
bury him. They no longer had thoughts of a
double-cross.

Sullivan was walking Lilian Blainey back to
the Bonne Chance. She said, 'Thank you for
the meal. That is a good restaurant. But you
know there were people there looking at us.
They are beginning to talk about the town
marshal picking up with a saloon girl.'

Sullivan corrected, 'Saloon singer.'

She smiled a little. 'It's all one to them.
The significant word is saloon.' She threw
him a curious glance. 'Do you intend to stay
a lawman all your life?'

He stopped walking and she halted with
him. He said thoughtfully, 'Now, that is a
question. I've done a lot of things – mining,
punching cows, railroad work – but this is
the one thing I've come to proper grips
with. I have sort of fitted into it. But now
you come to mention it there are other
things.' The smile had had a little less ice to
crack in his eyes lately.

She said hesitantly, 'If you thought of doing something else I thought I might mention that I – I have some considerable savings.' She gave a wry smile. 'Saloon work doesn't do much for your reputation but it does tend to fill the purse.' She flushed a little. 'I thought perhaps with whatever savings you might have and mine – we – you and I – might...?'

Sullivan gave her a long hard look. Then he took hold of her hand and raised it to his lips. He said, a little awkward with a woman for the first time in his life, 'I have never had a girl say something like that to me before.'

She blushed a little deeper. 'Is that your only answer?'

He looked up and down the street. There were a few people in sight here and there. He said, 'What the heck. This is my answer.'

Suddenly his arms were about her and his lips had found hers in a strong kiss of healthy passion. He felt her body yielding and the warm response of her lips to his. Then she pushed him back gently and turned to go into the saloon, her eyes just a trifle moist. Her voice was low. 'You could not have given me a better answer.'

Sullivan went back to his office. On the way he was thinking, if any drunken cowhand crosses my path tonight he's going to go scot-free. What a pity he hasn't got a girl like that.

Colonel Anastasio Roque de la Huerta spun around. There was a figure in his tent he had never seen before. It was a slim, dapper little man, neatly dressed and quiet. But there was something behind the quiet that told him he had better not bawl out for soldiers to come running. He spat out, 'Who are you? What is your business? How dare you—'

A toneless voice said coldly, 'Latour got your message about the big man and the cheaper offer he made to you about the cattle.'

The colonel started. He said, a little nervously, 'And?'

The man with the toneless voice said, 'It's all been fixed up. That offer no longer stands. You are back to paying twenty dollars a head to be handed over to Rance Horton on full delivery of the beeves.'

'Oh. I see.' The colonel tried to raise a little dignity. 'And who are you?'

The man turned towards the flap of the tent. 'Me? Why, I'm jest a messenger who brings you that news. I gave the big man another message. Jest before he died. I guess

162

you better take heed of that in case you are thinkin' of tryin' any Mexican fandango when it comes time for the payout. *Adios, señor.*'

As he went the colonel thought, with a slight shiver, he smells of the funeral parlour. But he is not the corpse. He is the one who puts corpses there.

THIRTEEN

Latour blew smoke from the cheroot. 'Fine. You have done splendidly, *mon ami. Magnifique*. But we have another problem.'

Kelso gave him his customary stare, a cold dead thing that chilled most of its recipients. 'And what might that be?'

The Frenchman took out a fancy handkerchief and flicked a touch of ash from his immaculate vest. He said briefly, 'The marshal. He has a very enquiring mind and he has been following things up like – how do you say it? – a hound dog on the scent of a raccoon.'

'So?'

Latour frowned. 'Theodora Cavendish has

163

been to see me.'

Kelso drawled with a touch of innuendo, 'That ain't new, boss.'

Latour raised an impatient hand. 'This was with information. Sullivan has already connected her up with our – ah – operation and it is obvious he has his eyes on me.'

The gunman asked smoothly, 'Has he spread the word?'

'I would think not. He is what you would call a cagey man. He will endeavour to get all his facts right before he brings it to the point of charging someone. But he needs to be stopped.' He murmured, *'Jusqu'au bout.'*

Kelso inquired easily, 'What was that bit of frog talk?'

The Frenchman smiled. 'I said, "to the very end".'

Kelso fingered his jaw. 'You are workin' this pistol of mine overtime.'

'You will be paid.' Latour paused. 'But I would suggest this must be done with – ah – discretion. From cover.'

Kelso bridled. 'You mean backshootin'. I ain't never done nothin' but face a man up – given him a chance to draw.'

Latour smiled. 'Even when he is drunk.' Kelso's eyes flashed quick resentment. The Frenchman smoothly pacified him. 'Now,

164

now, *mon ami*. This man is dangerous. I do not doubt your skill but in a shoot-out, who knows?' Kelso bridled again. Latour said soothingly, 'Luck can play a part in such an encounter. *Non, non*. This must be done from cover.'

Kelso relaxed, his eyes losing their momentary flicker of liveliness and reverting to their dead man's stare. 'OK, OK. When?'

'Soon, very soon.' He studied the gunman, smiling satisfiedly. 'I am only the *régisseur* but you are the *premier danseur*.'

'What's all that mean?'

Latour kept smiling. 'I am just the stage manager but you are the principal dancer.'

Kelso got up, hand flicking lightly to the gun on his right hip. 'Tell you somethin'. Sullivan won't be dancin' any more. Can't do it from a casket.'

Latour's smile grew wilder. A top gunhand was truly worth the hiring, expensive as it was.

Judge Achilles Archer made a gesture. 'This is my good friend, Henry Quincey, counsellor-at-law.' He nodded towards the boy. 'Henry, this is Jerome Owens, the lad I told you about.'

The lawyer, thin, angular, with pince-nez

sitting precariously on his nose, nodded and smiled. When he did that his face changed from that of a solemn owl to that of a kindly human being.

'Ah, yes. I heard about him before, of course. Went after those rustlers on his own. A trifle foolish but commendable, commendable.'

Jerry Owens, a little overcome, looked from one older man to the other and smiled uncertainly. The lawyer said briskly, 'Well, now, let's see. What interest do you have in the law, my boy?'

Jerry blinked. 'I sure like to keep it and to see it's being kept.'

'Admirable, admirable. Of course, you are referring to the – ah – rather robust activity of enforcing the law as a peace officer. But how do you view it otherwise?'

Jerry looked bewildered. 'I guess I don't know what you mean, sir.' The lawyer smiled again. Jerry liked him when he did that.

Henry Quincey sat back, touching his fingertips together in the manner of men of his profession. 'Young man, I am referring to the matter of interpreting the law for the benefit of those who may be in trouble and require legal assistance. I am alluding to the court-room, to judges and magistrates, to juries. I am talking about the profession which Cicero defined as a correct principle drawn from the inspiration of the gods, commanding what is honest and forbidding the contrary.'

Jerry Owens licked his lips nervously. 'Sir, I don't quite figure what you mean but it sounds awful important.'

Henry Quincey leaned towards him, his smile gone, his face all earnest solemnity. 'It *is* important, my boy, and increasingly important to this part of our nation, the frontier, the far west. The law as yet is only in its infancy out here. It needs to grow in its influence, to be recognized and practised in all its strength and to be supported wholeheartedly by all the citizens.'

He added drily, 'And then there will be far less need for dead-shot marshals and rough enforcement of law by virtue of the gun. Lynch parties will disappear and big ranchers will be stopped from denying their land and water rights to homesteaders. And decent women will be able to walk the streets of any western town after nightfall in safety and peace.'

The boy's eyes held a glimmer of appreciation. 'Gosh, sir, that sounds just like my ma talking, having been a schoolmarm and all.'

Henry Quincey smiled again, the crusader fierceness gone and the human warmth returning. He sat back. 'In short, boy, how would you like to be a lawyer?'

Judge Archer said firmly, 'He means, Jerome, that he is prepared to make out the papers to indenture you – to teach you how to be lawyer like himself.'

Jerry, speechless for the moment, nodded. Then suddenly he found voice. 'I'd – I'd like to talk it over with someone first.'

The judge's sober face broke into a smile. 'I guess you have my daughter in view. Well, let me tell you, young man, she has already made up her mind. She believes you ought to grab the chance with both hands.'

Jerry Owens' brain was whirling. He was thinking, from apprentice outlaw to apprentice peace officer to apprentice lawyer in mighty quick time. He suddenly felt very glad he had turned out of the wasteland the marshal had sent him into and headed back for Estrada.

Martin Sullivan was making his usual nightly patrol alone. He had not appointed any further deputies as yet. He was waiting to see when Jerry Owens was fit enough to take on his old job and he had no other prospective assistants in mind at the moment.

He had reached a shadowy part of the main street where lights hung up outside public places were absent and was automatically wary as he always had been when walking through any town in the shadows at night. He had almost passed the spot when the gun barked.

He went to the dirt in a hurry, the palms of his hands scratched by the gravel. Another shot spat up dirt close to his head.

But he had rolled over now and his own weapon was in his hand, plucked from the holster in one lightning grab. He fired twice in the direction the shots had come from but he could hear running footsteps and he knew that before he got to his feet the backshooter would be invisible.

It was the first time he had been fired on in that way in this town and he thought rapidly, it happens like that when people have the idea you are on their trail. He made for the Bonne Chance. Entering it, he made for Latour. He may have been mistaken but he fancied he saw a gleam of mixed surprise and shock on the Frenchman's face. It was gone in a moment, just like a school teacher with one fast movement rubs off a figure on a blackboard.

Sullivan asked calmly, 'That gunnie Kelso around?'

Latour glanced about him. 'I cannot see him, *m'sieur*. Why do you ask?'

Sullivan said, 'Just curious. Guess I'll take a look around.' He moved towards the back of the saloon, Latour gazing after him.

Sullivan looked quickly through the back rooms, one or two employees staring at him curiously, and then he came out and headed up the stairs leading from the end of the bar. He had reached the top landing when suddenly Kelso came out of a room.

Sullivan guessed he had come up the outside fire-escape stairs into that room he had just emerged from. He noted the gunman was breathing quickly.

Sullivan said quietly, 'You mind showing me that gun?'

Kelso's face was as expressionless as that of a cigar store Indian. 'No objections, Marshal.' He handed the pistol over. Sullivan broke it open and spun the chambers. They were all full and there was no smell of gunpowder.

He said curtly, 'Where's the other gun?'

Kelso said impassively, 'Only got one gun.'

Sullivan said, 'I hear tell you use two on occasions.'

Kelso shrugged. 'One's enough, Marshal. If you can't hit your target with one gun you won't do it with another.'

Sullivan handed the gun back. He said flatly, 'You have flim-flammed me one way or another tonight, Kelso. Maybe the other gun is in that room someplace or planted elsewhere. But I am not going to argue about that.' He fixed the man with a stare in which the ice had fully covered his eyes, making them look like frozen blue marbles. 'I've got this to say, Kelso, and I won't say it again. I want you out of this town and I want you out pronto. Tomorrow morning is soon enough but if you are not gone by then I am coming around to see that you are. And I am not going to be too careful how I do that.'

He turned and walked back down the stairs. As he passed Latour he said off-handedly, 'You are going to be one employee the less as of tomorrow, *m'sieur*. If I were you I would not encourage him to stay.'

Latour stared, unsmiling. As the stage manager he would have to arrange another little scene.

Occasionally they met in Doctor Freeman's surgery. The doctor had become a good friend of the marshal and he also liked Lilian Blainey. They entered different ways to avoid the appearance, for Latour's sake, of being too closely allied.

The girl said concernedly, 'Now that they know you have the rustling operation pretty well worked out they are going to be even more dangerous. There might be more pot-shots at you from alleyways at night.'

Sullivan grimaced. 'Not so likely with Kelso out of town. Saw him ride out this morning. Latour hasn't got time to hire another gunnie in a hurry.'

The girl was worried. 'Maybe he'll try something himself.'

'Hardly think so. He's the big operator behind the scenes. He pays other people to do the grubby work for him.'

She insisted, 'Watch him. Watch him closely. I'll do the same. I'll keep on being your eyes and ears around the Bonne Chance.'

Sullivan gave her a sudden smile. 'Don't make that contact too close. I guess I've got a prior claim.'

She smiled back at him. 'He's given up trying to maul me. But mind what I said. Latour is one Frenchman they should have kept in France. Preferably in the Bastille.'

Her face sobered. 'With all you know now, why aren't you closing in on him?'

He said shortly, 'I want to catch them in the act. Find the exact place they've driven the cattle to and move in when they are about to clinch the deal with whoever the buyers are.'

She said, anxiety in her voice, 'That could be very dangerous. There's bound to be shooting.'

He said cheerfully, 'Well, they've lost their best marksman.'

'I wouldn't be too sure. Bad pennies have a way of turning up again.'

'If he does he may find himself doing a sundance from the end of a rope.' He warmed her with a look. 'Just before you go–' She came across the floor of the room and into his arms. He kissed her in a long, warm embrace. 'If they lay a finger on you at any time–'

She moved gently back from him. 'More likely on you and more likely a trigger finger. Watch yourself. You're the only marshal I've got.'

Later he kept wondering how it was that this girl had come into his life when he had become disillusioned about women. Well, she had put all that out of his head and all he could think of now was to pick out some place where they could be together all the time for good.

The thought crossed his mind that a bullet was never far away in his line of work but he shrugged it off. He had dodged a lot of bullets in his time and he intended to keep on doing it.

Latour rode up to the cave mouth and called the other man's name.

After a moment or two Kelso came out. His horse, picketed to the right from the cave's opening, was grazing quietly. Latour dismounted. He said briefly, 'Tomorrow night. Come there and leave your horse handy. Sullivan has told me he wants to ask me a few questions. He asked me to meet him at a neutral place, an eating place he goes to. I believe he thinks he might be able to wheedle out of me where the cattle are taken to.'

Kelso said, 'Gittin' awful close to nabbin' you.'

Latour gritted his teeth.

'*Certainement.*'

'Well, what's the set-up?'

The Frenchman's eyes glared. 'I have found he always sits at a table near a window. At that range you should have no trouble.' He spelled out details.

Kelso's expressionless face showed a flicker of emotion – a sharp vengefulness. 'I owe that lawman.'

Latour turned to his horse. 'Till tomorrow night then, *au 'voir.*'

They had been seated at the table and started the meal. Sullivan was about to launch into the leading questions when Lilian Blainey came into the restaurant.

The marshal looked up, surprised. The girl came over towards them, smiling. She said pleasantly, 'Well, well, gentlemen, fancy seeing–'

At the same moment, still standing up, she caught the glimpse of movement through the window. In a flash she thrust a hand into a pocket in her frock and whipped out the derringer. She fired just prior to the thunder of the .44 from the other side of the window.

The slug from the .44 flew between Latour and the marshal, boring through the opposite wall. There was a thud from the other side of the window. Sullivan raced out, his own pistol in hand. He came back to find Lilian Blainey with the derringer, three shots still not fired, and holding it on a vastly discomfited Latour. She said calmly to the marshal, 'Thought you might need some back-up.'

Sullivan shook his head, a grim smile dawning on his face. 'Don't you ever train that thing on me. Gil Kelso is out there with a hole in his head that might have been bored by an auger. Saved us some time in court.'

He fixed his gaze on the Frenchman. 'You have a whole lot more explaining to do now, Latour. But somehow I don't think anyone is going to listen much.'

FOURTEEN

Sullivan had ridden out to the Slash C in a hurry. Theodora Cavendish faced him across the rug-strewn length of the living-room her ex-husband Curly had made so lavish for her.

Her eyes were flashing defiance. 'What do you mean, leave?' She flung out her hand in a gesture to take in all around her. 'This is my home. It suits me. I like it very much. Why should I leave?'

Sullivan rapped, 'Kings have had to leave palaces when the throne got a little hot for them. What I am telling you, black-haired lady, is that a real rip-roaring prairie fire is building up around you. Once everyone gets to know how big a hand you have had in this rustling you are likely to become the first female I've heard of lynched by a mob.'

She threw him a provocative look, a dark smile on her lips. 'You'd save me.'

He shook his head. 'Not any more, Theodora. You wove your little spell on me and for a while it was pretty nice. But I burst the net and what we had is through. You are strictly on your own from this point on.' He corrected himself. 'Still, I guess that won't be for long with that body, that hair and those eyes.'

She became imploring. 'You can't mean this – surely there's some way ...?

Sullivan said wearily, 'I seem to have spent a lot of time telling people to get out of this town and not to keep meddling the way they were doing. Two of them didn't pay much attention and now they are both dead. You get my drift?'

She hesitated. 'This is your last word?'

He said pointedly, 'The very last. I'm giving you this chance because, well, we did have something going at one time.' His eyes held a touch of cynicism. 'Although you always had something in reserve, didn't you?' He threw his arm around in a wide sweep. 'Maybe out there you'll find someone for whom you won't be able to keep it back. The world's a big place, Theodora. Find somewhere to disappear to. Maybe with a new name.'

She was silent for a moment or two. A faint smile crossed her face. 'Maybe I will.'

She came across the room and placed her hands on his shoulders. She reached up a little and kissed him on the lips. 'That's for the memory, Marshal.'

When he was riding away he thought how that even when she was standing in front of him, like some dark enchantress of the night, the blonde head of Lilian Blainey shut her out like the sun did the moon. That was the girl for him when it was all over.

He thought grimly, it wasn't over yet by a long way and he hoped his luck in dodging flying lead was going to hold.

Sullivan rode at the head of them. They were a big mixed cavalcade, bosses and their ramrods and range riders from all over. It was the biggest posse he had ever led. Each one represented ranches from which cattle had been stolen and they had blood in their eyes as they rode out.

All of them were determined not only to get their stolen beasts back but to make the robbers pay.

Sullivan had tried to figure out how many there would be facing them when they got there. He knew now to where the rustled cows had finally been driven and he also knew a little about Rance Horton. He had found out Horton had been a cheating gambler who had been involved in several shootings with men who had not liked the way he had played. That Horton was still alive and his accusers were not indicated that he could clearly be termed a dangerous man.

The marshal roughly calculated the number of guns there would be waiting for them. There were the Palmers and the several Slash C gunnies Theodora had hired. Also there would be the ones Latour had taken on apart from the now deceased Kelso and Horton's own few tough gunhands he would need around him to help keep his own affairs in order. But hardly as many as the pursuing posse.

Still, all of the rustlers, Sullivan guessed,

would be gathered at the Horton spread, waiting for the big payout as the cattle were passed on to the buyers. There had been no rustling done for a while and he sensed the lull would have indicated the end of the raids.

By now, he had figured, the final round-up of rustled animals would be getting close to their destination at the Horton ranch. Maybe the buyers were some shady dealers whom Latour and Horton had lined up in advance. Whoever they were they were going to find plenty of lead flying their way.

He pushed on. One more campfire and they would be there.

When they came up on the verge of the sprawling ranchland Sullivan called a halt. He beckoned one of the ranchers. 'Pete Donovan, we've got to send a couple of riders in to take a good look around. You got anyone could do it?'

The rancher, face weathered into hard grooves by years of facing sun and sand, dust storms and blizzards, nodded curtly. 'Got a Injun and another feller who useta scout for the army.'

The marshal clipped, 'Good. Send them off while we wait around.' The rancher rode back to a bunch of men and detailed a couple. They rode off in a hurry. The waiting riders slouched in the saddle, staring after them with cold, intent gaze.

After a while the two riders re-emerged from back across a slope they had ridden over. Sullivan and their boss went to meet them. The white rider with the keen, slit eyes of a former scout drawled, 'They is more cows over that hill than I ever see'd at a railhead.' He looked at Donovan. 'See'd a couple with our Rockin' D brand still on 'em, boss.' The rancher scowled.

The rider went on, 'They's a big ranch house, a bunkhouse an' barn. Corrals for a big remuda. Some men around. Not a awful lot. Guess there's maybe more.'

The Indian added, 'Can't tell.' He grinned. 'But plenty shooting when we go in.'

Sullivan snapped, 'Anything else?'

The rider who had been an army scout said easily, 'Yeah. A big somethin' else. They is near as many Mex sojers on the other side of the ranch as they is cows. All wearin' them red jackets of them *rurales*. Could be rebels turned agin the gov'ment. Lookin' sorta hungry.'

Sullivan drew in a long breath. 'So they're the buyers. Rebel troops looking for beef.'

The rancher bit out, 'Beef they ain't gunna git.'

Sullivan was wary. 'Let's not get carried away on this, Pete. They could be a hard nut to crack. Some of them will be experienced gun-fighters and we don't have an awful lot of them among our boys.'

The rancher was emphatic. 'They all know how to fight an' even cowhands can git riled up about their bosses' beeves bein' stole. Rustlers are a dirty breed to all honest cowpunchers.'

The marshal raised a hand. 'OK, Pete, I get your point. Now, look, we can't afford to just ride in. As soon as they see us they'll know what we've come about. We've got to ride up as easy-like as we can and then start shooting.'

The rancher put his hand on the rifle in his saddle boot. 'Jest let's git started.'

The group came together and at Sullivan's signal they began moving towards the slope the two scouts had just ridden back from. The other side of it they were in full view of anyone at the buildings now facing them.

Sullivan's eyes took in the whole scene before them. It was just as Donovan's two riders had said – sprawling buildings, corrals full of horses that had been hard ridden and several men walking around who even at that distance could be seen to be tough and wiry. One of these men suddenly pointed at the oncoming riders and raised a shout. Those with him jerked their heads around to look and started running for the nearest building.

Pete Donovan quickly drew his rifle from the boot, levelled it and fired.

One of the running men fell, obviously shot in the leg. A couple more cowpunchers around Donovan started shooting.

The men fired at kept running for the buildings, leaving their shot companion behind. He hobbled to his feet but before he could start limping after the other men another shot rang out from Pete Donovan's rifle. The man fell, obviously dead. The rancher grated, 'May the crows pick your eyes out, cow thief.'

As the running men reached the nearest building a burst of fire came from their direction, a couple of rifles cracking. A man in the ranchers' group cried out as a bullet tore through his shoulder. Sullivan yelled, 'Go for cover.'

Where the posse had grouped there was a wide spread of live oak. They rode in amongst it, sheltering behind the massive trees covered with moss. They left their mounts and became sharpshooters on foot, using the trees as protection.

The shooting from both sides had now become heavy. Sullivan got up alongside Pete Donovan and a couple of other ranchers. He rapped, 'This will turn into a stand-off. They can't see us and we can't see them. We've got to get closer.'

Donovan muttered, 'Lotta lead comin' from their side.'

The marshal snapped, 'Got to get around 'em. I figure we outnumber them. By the amount of their fire I don't figure there's more than a dozen or so. I'll take a half dozen of our men to one side if you, Pete, take the same number to the opposite. There's cover on both sides. When they're getting fired on from three directions they might start to get thinking they are not in a healthy position. If we can drive them out of those buildings we'll have them on the run.'

He moved around quickly, calling a man here and there. Pete Donovan followed his lead, gathering together a group of men holding rifles in cool, experienced hands.

Dodging and running, the two groups made their way to opposite sides of the buildings. Combined with the rest of the posse in amongst the big oaks, they poured a heavy, ceaseless fire into the buildings.

After a while the firing from the ranch house, where most of the rustlers seemed to be gathered, became less, more sporadic. Sullivan exulted, 'They are getting hit. Keep it up, boys.'

Suddenly a figure was seen to emerge from the big building. Running swiftly, he was headed for one of the corrals. A voice yelled at him from inside the ranch house but he kept running. A sudden shot fired from the ranchhouse itself hit him. The man dropped and lay still. The marshal's voice was cold and hard. 'Trying to run out on 'em. One of his friends, maybe Horton, didn't like it. When they start shooting each other down we've really got them on the move.'

The posse kept pouring in their heavy fire. The return volleys from the ranch house were definitely slowing down now, their intensity much less. Some members of the posse began to slacken their fire. The marshal's voice was loud and insistent. 'Don't slow down! Keep pouring it into them.'

The fire power of the posse picked up again. Suddenly something was poked through a window of the ranch house. It was a white rag on a stick being waved from side to side.

Sullivan stood up and yelled, 'If you mean that come on out with your hands up.'

There was silence and then a faint sound of movement from inside the ranch house. A couple of figures appeared, another limping behind them, dragging a wounded leg.

Two more figures came out from the barn on which fire had also been directed, one man's arm hanging uselessly. Other figures appeared until there was a few more than a dozen gathered outside the buildings.

Sullivan went over to them warily, rifle at the ready. Nearing the group, he called, 'That all of you that were in there?'

A voice said sourly, 'All but three. They're dead.'

Pete Donovan's voice said next to Sullivan. 'Our three wounded ain't so bad then.'

Sullivan was searching the men with his eyes. His glance fell on an angular bony man with the look of leadership about him. Behind his expressionless face Sullivan sensed a seething anger at what had happened. The marshal asked abruptly, 'You Horton?'

The man flickered a scowl in reply. 'So what?'

Sullivan said, 'Just wanted your confirmation.' He added, 'Looks like you're the one who really might be swinging from a rope's end.'

When the posse had emerged from the trees and the rustlers all made captive, Sullivan pointed to the cows spread out across the range. 'Better round them up. That's what we came for.'

All this time there had been no movement from the Mexican soldiery gathered on the far side of the ranch. Sullivan looked back towards them as he and the rest of the posse gathered the cavalcade of cattle and horses, also mostly stolen he figured, to head back north.

Suddenly a small group of riders left the Mexican camp and began to ride towards the marshal and the posse. Sullivan signalled Pete Donovan and a couple of the other ranchers to join him as he turned to meet the Mexicans.

The soldiers pulled up as they met the marshal and the ranchers face to face. The Mexicans' leader was a slender man with a blaze of medals across his chest and the look, thought Sullivan, of a lean-ribbed coyote wanting to be the leader of a big pack. He spoke first in broken English. '*Señor*, where are you taking these cows?'

Sullivan answered him in fluent Spanish

187

he had picked up from years in the south-west and giving the man his proper rank. 'We are taking them home, Colonel – to where they came from. They were stolen.'

Colonel de la Huerta's face showed appreciation of the use of his native tongue. Not exactly Castilian but good enough. 'To save you the trouble of herding them all the way back we will give you twelve dollars a head for them.'

Sullivan shook his head. 'They're worth twenty a head. No sale, Colonel.'

The colonel made another offer. 'Fifteen dollars per head and that is our top price.'

Sullivan again shook his head. 'Won't take all that long to get them back. A little slow but we'll get there. And when these cows pick up a little after the way they've been driven around they will fetch twenty dollars a head easy.'

The colonel was silent. Then he looked back towards the main body of his troops. He said as if musing aloud, 'I have a large number of soldiers, *señor*. A lot of fire power. Can we not persuade you?'

Sullivan sat loosely in the saddle, calm and still. 'Colonel, this could turn into a border incident involving your country and ours. Surely we don't want that. Just let us be on our way and forget the bargaining, huh?'

De la Huerta stared at him, eyes almost as icy as Sullivan at his coldest. Suddenly he turned his horse away back towards his camp. 'Very well, *señor*. *Adios*, and good travelling.'

As the colonel rode back with his small group around him Sullivan said to Pete Donovan and the others, 'That is not the last we are going to see of them. And I'll tell you something else. Horton and Latour would have been lucky to see that money. That colonel has the look of an *hombre* who would have murdered the rustlers and taken the cows for free. We had better post good lookouts.'

They rode on with grim faces but Sullivan knew these tough ranchers and their weatherbeaten riders were going to take a lot of prising loose from their cows.

FIFTEEN

Sullivan had arranged things like a military encampment. He had the prisoners roped together in the centre of a big square, a couple of cowhands with rifles standing guard over them. The cattle had several men riding herd on them, the extra horses they had picked up at the Horton ranch roped off with the posse's own mounts.

When the men bedded down for the night he had them spread out in a circle that enclosed the whole camp. He had instructed them all to have their weapons ready and to be up and shooting at a moment's notice. He had told every man who changed with others on night herd to keep a rifle in their saddle boot.

Pete Donovan had asked a little dubiously, 'You figger them greasers will try to jump us?'

Sullivan was emphatic. 'Nothing surer. They are hungry. They want those beeves. And we are not yet far away from the border. Another day or two we will be and they won't want to chase us that far. But what right now we have to expect is an attack, probably a surprise one at night, to take those cows off our hands and to shoot anyone who gets in their way. What we have to do is shoot first and give them a barrage that will drive them off. Remember, it took four thousand of them at the Alamo to beat a hundred and eighty Texans. The odds will be a little better than that this time, even if the colonel sends all his troops, which I don't think he will.' He added uncertainly, 'I'm just a little worried the shooting might spook the animals.'

Later on the riders on night herd were singing softly to the cattle and a few lying down on the hard earth on the perimeter of the camp were dozing a little. Sullivan himself and a handful of hard-headed ranchers determined to keep their cows now they had got them back were sitting up and wide awake.

When the Mexicans struck it was with a cavalry charge out of the night. They evidently intended to do their best to put paid to the posse before turning their attention to the cows.

Sullivan was up on his feet in a flash and yelling to all the members of the posse to open fire. The Mexicans, taken by surprise by the unexpected fury and force of the counter attack, were forced to swerve aside in their gallop, regroup, and charge again.

This time the Americans' fire was even thicker and more deadly. Several Mexican saddles were emptied, the riderless horses running off wildly. In the mêlée men on foot were to be seen moving frantically amongst the gunfire and the charging animals.

The posse increased their fire, pouring hot lead into the red-jacketed horsemen. Suddenly the attacking riders wavered. Then they broke and turned and galloped off.

The Americans gave them a final furious burst. Sullivan grinned, relaxing a little. He looked anxiously towards the cattle. They were milling about and lowing loudly and a couple of the night herd riders were pushing a few back that had begun to gallop off but there was not going to be a stampede.

Sullivan let out a long sigh. 'First time I saw it like that when cows got startled at night. The good Lord must be with us.' He began to walk around. 'Anyone hurt?'

There came cries of reassurance from all over. One husky voiced cowhand bawled, 'They was not shootin' much. Only ridin'. Figgered my only chance of gittin' wounded was to have a horse step on me.' Another agreed. 'You're right, boy. But they never got close enough for that.'

Sullivan, joined by a couple of the older and more cautious ranchers, kept on walking about, checking on things. A cowboy who had been one of the two guarding the roped and tied captives came up breathlessly. 'Marshal, that feller Horton – figger he's gone.'

Another cowhand joined them. 'Yeah, Marshal, when we was shootin' at the greasers and a couple was knocked off their hosses I seen a feller out there without one of them fancy rigs they was wearin' an' he grabbed a hoss an' bolted on it. Musta been that Horton *hombre.*'

Sullivan cursed. 'How'd he get free?'

The first cowboy offered, 'Well, maybe he had a knife somewhere on him we missed findin'. Guess he cut the rope an' skedaddled. We was all too busy shootin' at them Mex sojers to notice.'

Sullivan rasped, 'Well, why didn't more of them get loose?'

Pete Donovan offered, 'Guess they didn't fancy runnin' out there with all the lead that was flyin'. That Horton, crook an' all as he is, must be a pretty nervy character.'

Sullivan was brief. 'Well, I'll have to go get him.'

Pete Donovan stared. 'You – alone?'

The marshal nodded. 'Yes. It'll need all of you to get everything back home nice and tidy. Don't want to take anyone else away from that job.'

Donovan queried, 'But why? Why not let the buzzard go? We got everyone and everything else.'

Sullivan's jaw set and if Pete Donovan could have seen his eyes in the dark he would have been surprised at the icicles that now glittered there.

'The rest are only hired hands. Horton was in on the whole box and dice. He was a leading figure in the whole crooked deal – the only one who is left to bring in. I'll get him put on trial if it's the last thing I do.'

He swung around on the cowhand who had seen Horton escape. 'Which way did he head off?'

'I'd say north-west, Marshal. Forkin' left from the way we are headin'.'

Sullivan thought aloud. 'Likely heading for a town and a change of horses. Betting is that he is wearing a body belt with money in it. All we searched them for was weapons. The quicker I go the quicker I'll catch up with him.'

Donovan jerked out, 'You leavin' right

now? Can't see tracks in the dark.'

'Don't have to. There's a town called Black Bear Creek I figure he might be riding towards. Reckon if I head for there I'll catch up with him pretty soon.'

Pete Donovan drawled, 'Yeah, well, that mountain of a horse you ride oughta soon run down a Mex mustang.'

'Maybe so. But I won't be flogging my mount like he will his. But we'll catch up with him soon enough.'

Donovan went on, 'It's jest that when you catch him up it could be a mite tricky. That man struck me as bein' a sorta hard man when closed off in a corner. Sure you don't want no help?'

Sullivan demurred. 'Head up the whole shebang and take them home, Pete. Pretty sure the Mex soldiers won't try to jump you again. They got their bellies too full of lead this time.'

When he was mounted on the big black horse again he headed for Black Bear Creek. A cornered Horton would, as Pete Donovan had said, be a mite tricky. He would do his best to make sure it did not end up with Lilian Blainey in mourning.

Sullivan rode into town on the horse he

called Ace, alert, wary, narrow-eyed.

He passed down the main street and eyed off the several saloons. He picked one out that looked about the most promising, hitched the black to the rail outside and went in.

After he had asked about Horton, describing him as best he could, the barman eyed him cautiously. 'You a lawman, ain't you?'

The marshal assented. The barman hesitated. 'This here jasper you asked about – what's he done?'

Sullivan judged the man to be honest, almost certainly a family man whose kids he was trying to raise right. The marshal said, 'Rustling – on a big scale. He is a very dishonest man.'

The barman wagged his head. 'That's bad. Y'know, there's a lot of badness around. But, you see, I wanted to make sure I wasn't informing on someone who was being harassed unfairly, you know, being chased for something he didn't do or for something small that some peace officers would turn a blind eye to.'

He placed a glass he was polishing on a shelf behind him. 'Well, I'll tell you, sir. There was a feller who sure fits your description came in here and had a drink or two.' He picked up another glass. 'Asked where he could buy a horse. Wanted to change the one he had. Seems he had been travelling mighty hard on it.'

Sullivan interjected. 'Did he look as if he thought he was being followed?'

The man thought a minute. 'No, sir. He didn't have a hunted look. I've seen men on the run before and this one was breathing kind of easy. Maybe he figured if anyone was chasing him he'd shaken them off.'

Sullivan urged, 'Well, what then?'

'I told him to see Nevada Slim, best horse dealer around.'

'Where will I find him?'

'Down the main street a piece on this side. Got a livery down there.'

Nevada Slim was a thin, old man with a bent back and an eye that glittered like a thieving magpie. When Sullivan flashed his badge the old man was co-operative. He drawled, 'The critter he wanted me to take was beat up. Been ridin' it hard a long ways. Had a big heavy Mex saddle on it.' He rolled his bird-sharp eyes heavenward. 'Sure hope it wasn't stole.'

Sullivan said drily, 'I don't believe that would give you a bad case of insomnia. Anything else you can tell me?'

The old man looked cunning. 'Well, now, Marshal, age has come upon me an' my mem'ree–'

Sullivan tossed him a coin. 'Here's a memory pill.'

The old man brightened. 'Wanted to know a store where he could best buy some provisions, a bed roll, a pistol an' some cartridges.' He said self-righteously, 'Might jest say that I sold him a hoss that was bigger an' pacier than the one he traded in. An' for a mighty fair price.'

'Did you see him leave?'

'Sure did. Headed direct north. Wasn't 'zackly hustlin' the beast along but he wasn't wastin' any time, neither.'

'How long ago?'

'This very mornin'. Left here maybe an hour or two past.' He threw a sharp eye over Sullivan's big black. 'But I figger if you are chasin' him on that elephant you oughta catch up with him right soon. Looks like a mighty big-steppin' animal.'

'It is. Thanks, oldtimer. We'll be on our way.' In the saddle and headed out of town his mind was turning over. Looked like Horton thought he was free of any likely pursuers and was not avoiding towns but while keeping up a steady pace was moving from one town to another to his final destination.

Sullivan thought it was likely he was headed back for the gaming tables of 'Frisco. Much would have died down since he was last there.

It was that night he caught up with Horton. The bony man had made a leisurely camp for the night before moving on to the next town which was within easy reach for about noon the next day.

Sullivan left the black with the reins trailing, knowing that the big horse would not move until he came back or called the animal. He crept on silently and stepped out of the shadows into the light of the fire. Horton, startled, looked up, reaching for his gun.

Sullivan, gun already in hand, said evenly, 'I wouldn't try that. You are a great target against that firelight.'

Horton paused and drew his hand back. His voice was flat and calm, that of a card player who never showed his emotions. 'Looks like you've outplayed my hand, Marshal.'

'Appears so. Now, we'll just sit around a while and I'll help you drink that coffee. Then I'll tie your wrists and ankles and we'll bed down for the night before we head off for Estrada.'

After he had trussed up the man who now answered him only in monosyllables Sullivan whistled for the horse. The big animal came up immediately and Sullivan picketed him near to Horton's own grazing animal. He said, 'You were heading north but come the morning we'll be heading east for Estrada. I'm going to loosen your legs now and I'll spread out your bedroll for you and let you roll up in your blanket before I tie your legs again. I'll be sleeping nearby with one eye on you.' He said casually, 'I saw a feller once in a travelling show who got out of ropes like that in a hurry but I don't figure you have his knowhow. Anyway, I'm so light a sleeper that a kitten walking over a fur rug would wake me. Just go to sleep and forget about it, Horton.'

The bony man remained silent. His eyes seem to have sunk back even a little more into his cadaverous face. A thought passed through Sullivan's mind that an opposing card player looking at Horton's eyes to figure out what kind of a hand he was holding would have looked in vain.

The marshal went to his own blanket spread on top of his slicker and rolled himself in it. The pistol he had taken from

Horton lay at his head next to his own .44. If the bony man tried anything he may have to make it unnecessary for him to appear in court.

It was when Sullivan was going to make camp for the next night that it happened.

For the purposes of Horton riding his own horse and handling it himself, the marshal had first untied his legs and then tied his hands together at the front instead of at the back.

When they pulled up and Horton got down off his horse Sullivan untied his hands preparatory to retying them behind him.

Horton said mildly, 'Like to get some grain from my saddle-bag for my horse.'

The marshal stood back a little. 'Nice to see you have a mind for the animal.' Then he had quick second thoughts and went to draw his own weapon. But already Horton's hand had gone down into the saddle-bag and had come up with the derringer held straight at the marshal.

The man who looked more like an undertaker than a gambler said quietly, 'Good to have a hide gun stashed away somewhere apart from your body. Now, just step right back, Marshal.'

Sullivan was telling himself that must have been an extra purchase back there in the place where Horton had changed horses. He was a cagey man who prepared himself for any situation.

Horton quickly remounted his horse. 'Maybe I ought to shoot you down right here and now but I don't want to go up for murder. But hear this, Marshal. If you keep following me I'll be waiting for you and I will kill you dead sure. Just hand me that .44 you took from me and also pass me up your rifle, your cartridge belt and your pistol.'

Silently the marshal fumbled with his gunbelt as he handed to the other man his weapons and ammunition. Standing back, he asked quietly, 'Let me keep the pistol, Horton. I might meet up with bad company on the road and even an empty weapon is some defence.'

The gambler stared back at him unblinkingly, eyes slits of calculation. Finally he shrugged. 'I should leave you unarmed and at anyone's mercy but what the heck?' He threw the pistol back to Sullivan, carefully emptying it before he did.

When he had galloped off, the marshal bent down to the ground and retrieved the one bullet he had managed to remove from the gunbelt while fumbling with it to pass up to Horton. One shot. When he caught up with Horton again it had better not miss.

Sullivan had glimpsed the creek and from the distance Horton riding his horse down to it. He didn't appreciate the lack of cover he had as the other man threw a quick look behind him but he figured it was just a speedy glance and Horton had not seen him, he hoped.

As he approached the trees spread out along the edge of the creek he quickly dismounted and went ahead on foot. He had covered only a few cautious yards when Horton's voice rapped, 'Stay right there, lawman.'

Sullivan froze. This man was cagier than he had already given evidence of. He had evidently seen the marshal coming and had left his own horse by the stream and had backtracked. He came into full view.

'This looks like it, Marshal. You are a bloodhound I need to put off my trail for good. Don't say I didn't tell you this. Now, if I aim at that second top button on your shirt it ought to–'

There were two shots, the bony man's just slightly preceding Sullivan's. But the marshal had spun his body sideways, flipped the gun into his hand and fired all in one eye-dazzling movement.

Sullivan looked at his own left shoulder. There was a ragged tear in his shirt sleeve and a scarlet graze underneath.

He switched his gaze to Horton. The gambler was falling forward like a hobo who had been thrown off a box car. There was a black-rimmed hole in his chest that was slowly turning red. He hit the ground and became motionless.

Sullivan thought, I'll be riding back to Estrada alone. You can't call a corpse company.

The judge glowered. 'It certainly doesn't pleasure me to know you are handing in your badge. Never seen a slicker job done than the way you rounded up these cow thieves.' He fixed the marshal with a fierce glare. 'The Cavendish woman got away but that judge who held trial on Latour certainly fixed that conniving Frenchman. By the time he gets out of prison the fashions will have changed in Paris ten times. You tell me this lawman friend of yours will be a good replacement. Tell me, is he a really straight man?'

'So straight, Judge, he would make a gun

barrel look crooked. He has tamed a town or two in his time and he's ready to come. I took the liberty of writing him a little while ago when I was thinking of making this move.'

'H'mph.' He threw the next sentence at the marshal grumpily. 'So you are going to marry this saloon girl and settle some place else?'

Sullivan smiled bleakly. 'You know how it is, Judge. A peace officer marrying a girl who worked in a saloon. Too many refined people in Estrada might not like it. We'll probably buy up a little spread somewhere or maybe a store and set to making it pay.'

The judge thrust out his hand. 'Martin, you're all I ever told them here you would be. Good luck wherever you go and whatever you do.'

Down at the stage Sadie Torrence thrust her head in the door of the coach with a triumphant smile and then looked back at the marshal mounted on the big black horse. 'Didn't I tell you they don't come no better than some saloon girls?'

'You sure did, Sadie. And you were dead right.' The blonde-haired girl in the coach smiled up at him.

Jerry Owens and Faith Archer waved as

they left, Sullivan moving alongside the stage on the big black horse. Jerry spoke up. 'I don't figure they'll ever be going to court to bust up *that* marriage.'

Faith smiled. 'Seeing that the judge tied the knot I don't believe they would dare.' They went off together hand in hand.

The publishers hope that this book has given you enjoyable reading. Large Print Books are especially designed to be as easy to see and hold as possible. If you wish a complete list of our books please ask at your local library or write directly to:

Dales Large Print Books
Magna House, Long Preston,
Skipton, North Yorkshire.
BD23 4ND

This Large Print Book, for people
who cannot read normal print,
is published under the auspices of

THE ULVERSCROFT FOUNDATION